THE SULTAN OF
MONTE CRISTO

THE SULTAN OF
MONTE CRISTO

The First Sequel to
the Count of Monte Cristo

HOLY GHOST WRITER

Library of Congress Control Number: 2012910885
ISBN: Hardcover   978-1-4771-3020-9
                     Softcover   978-1-4771-3019-3
                     eBook   978-1-4771-3021-6

Rev. date: 12/03/2013

Contents

The Sultan of Monte Cristo had me hooked from the beginning to the very last word. It is a brilliant piece of living art that jumps off the page. This book is written so well, and the description is so vivid I felt like I belonged in that day and age. If there is a book to read and re-read over and over again, The Sultan of Monte Cristo is a story wherein you can do just that.

The author brings absolute magic to the reader and I couldn't think of anyone else who could have written this sequel other than Holy Ghost Writer.

Epic Reviews

INTRODUCTION

IT FELT SAD. It was like saying "goodbye" to a dear friend, when reading the last words, "wait and hope," of the 1,243-page book, *The Count of Monte Cristo*.

How long is the reader willing to wait and hope, to learn what became of Edmond Dantes, Haydee, Mercedes, the Morrels, the Danglars or the Villeforts, after putting down the book?

One need wonder no longer, as *The Sultan of Monte Cristo* unfolds in the spirit of Alexandre Dumas – the spirit that creates in its readers a hunger and a thirst for literature.

This sequel picks up in the 1840s, when Dumas is working as an investigative reporter, and publishes *The Count of Monte Cristo*. Like a true account of a real-life Edmond Dantes, that book serves as a point of reference for both original and new characters in the ongoing saga.

While new characters are introduced in the second chapter, the first significant new character is not introduced until the eighth chapter, in the person of Raymee.

Raymee's introduction is similar to that of Vampa early in *The Count of Monte Cristo*, but Raymee plays a more significant role.

The Count of Monte Cristo is one of history's best-known stories, and reading or re-familiarizing oneself with the original text, or a good translation thereof, will bring about the best result in understanding the references and characters developed in this sequel. However, this sequel (and subsequent sequels) can be enjoyed without a familiarity with the original work.

Countless readers over many generations have found the drama of a man unjustly imprisoned and emerging unrecognized, only to stealthily take revenge, to be a compelling and relevant story. Knowledge of a hidden treasure, provided to the Count of Monte Cristo by an elderly, long-bearded prisoner, makes the original a story that is entirely appropriate and exciting for even young children. However, *The Sultan of Monte Cristo* is a little too risqué for a very young audience, and is recommended for those at least 18 years of age.

This sequel, based on a true story, is made that much more compelling in this age when one considers that 65 million Americans, according to a recent article in *USA Today*, have already been convicted of a crime. One can easily imagine that some percentage of those are innocent and suffer as equally as Edmond Dantes did; they may even be experiencing their own thoughts and plans of revenge.

However, the fruits of revenge are not what we expect them to be. In future sequels, Edmond Dantes, deeply repentant for the unintended consequences of his revenge in the original story, will realize as the poet Milton observed, that revenge – though sweet at first – will before long recoil on its victor.

Readers may speculate that the Holy Ghost Writer qualifies as a true successor to Dumas; yet concomitantly, it has been inferred that he is an individual who has emerged from prison as a type of adventurous character in his own life, perhaps wishing to conceal his true identity by writing under the ghostly pen name. The true identity of the HGW will become known, once he interacts under his real name with the fictitious characters in one of the final books leading up to Book Ten. The publisher will give a prize to the first person who can discover, from the clues that will be planted throughout the ten books, his/her true identity. To submit your guess, email *prize@ sultanofmontecristo.com*.

Since the Count of Monte Cristo saw himself as divine providence, we speculate that the word "holy" in the Ghost Writer name was inspired by this fact; yet there are some unexpected twists in this sequel that may also contribute to the pseudonymous moniker.

Although plot shifts come unexpectedly in this sequel, they fit seamlessly and grow out of some small seeds planted in the original story that never took root therein. One of those small seeds is the word "hemp", found in the first chapters of the original story by Dumas. "Merovingian" is another one of those seeds, as Dumas referred to the youngest of those Merovingians as the "do nothing kings."

We call the original book by Dumas "Book I," and this first sequel, "Book II," with each chapter distinguished as "Count I," "Count II," etc.

There are ten counts, or chapters, in Book II, which will soon be followed by twelve more books (the sixth to be published next, entitled *That Girl Started Her Own Country*) that will continue into the twenty-first century, and then into the future (*The Boy Who Played with Dark Matter*, the eleventh book), featuring offspring of the Count of Monte Cristo. These sequels will take you places Dumas could have logically gone, but likely did not imagine.

BOOK II COUNT I

SINBAD THE SAILOR

AS EDMOND DANTES, KNOWN TO SOME AS SINBAD THE SAILOR, DISAPPEARS INTO THE SUNSET on his way to Albania, the last golden rays of the day shine on Haydee, giving her the appearance of a Greek goddess of beauty and love.

It isn't solely her charm and exquisite beauty that infatuate the Count of Monte Cristo, but that Haydee has confessed that she will die without him.

The reawakening of his former self as Edmond Dantes, resulting from that haunting visit to his dungeon on Chateau D'If, has given rise within him to questions of how long Haydee will wait if he were to disappear. Is she as weak and faithless as Mercedes? Should he put her to the test? His doubt torments him, for he deeply wishes that Haydee can be loyal and true, unwavering in her love despite any length of absence, in a way that Mercedes had not.

Haydee, however, has never doubted that she can wait until the end of time for her Edmond. She can anticipate his every need, after years of focusing her thoughts on how to please him. She understands that legally, she is only a slave, yet her savior has always treated her like a princess, making her love him all the more. Haydee realizes that her master, having avenged her parents' treacherous deaths and his own enemies' crimes, may have a difficult time closing that long chapter and moving on with life; she makes every effort to distract him and pull him into a happier future.

She moves to him, her hips swaying with a sensual grace, and rests her hand on his shoulder. "Lord, I have prepared a special dessert for you to take your mind off the past, hoping you will find my company worthy of your time and affection."

"My darling Haydee, true, noble, royal princess, I am all yours," Dantes replies, his thoughts elsewhere. "There is no one at whose side I'd rather spend my sunsets."

Haydee hesitates to speak her true fear, yet overcomes it – she has to know, though it will not alter her devotion to him in the slightest. "My Lord, I fear your heart forever belongs to Mercedes. Have you really forgiven her and let her go, now that your revenge is complete almost to the point of self-destruction?"

"My dear, adorable child, I went too far in my quest for justice and nearly lost my soul," Dantes answers, lifting his head to gaze upon her. "You are my salvation. Only since discovering your love for me is my heart beginning to mend."

"Dear Master, my sweet Sinbad, please do not call me 'child.' I am a woman now, with the same passion – no, with more passion – to be loved by you, than Mercedes had the day you were to be married, when she was my age. And you are still a young man, even though you have achieved twice my years. Revenge may have sacrificed your passion for love, but let me rekindle those flames. Tonight I will awaken that which years of isolation, followed by absorption in obsessive planning, withered in your heart."

Edmond Dantes begins to feel that icy part of his heart melting as his pulse quickens. Has he truly never noticed the slender beauty of Haydee's waist, the thick fall of her hair?

For the first time, Dantes truly sees her. "I promise to never call you 'child' again, because you have become my master and I am willingly your slave. Command me as if one of your servants. Since you have been restored to your hereditary throne, let me call you 'Sultana.' You, Haydee, are not just becoming the sovereign of a nation; you are the sovereign owner of my heart. I cannot in words express my gratitude for how you've stood beside me."

The Count of Monte Cristo reflects on how he has ruled the events of the past few years as if he were Providence itself, yet lost his confidence after the unintended consequences of the death of Édouard. A battle is raging in his mind. Is he Edmond Dantes, Sinbad the Sailor, the mysterious and powerful Count of Monte Cristo, or any of the other personages he created to bring about his vengeance? Can he go back to being simply Edmond Dantes, or is it his fate to metamorphosis into a new personality? No matter his fate, though, he can see that it is his destiny to have Haydee at his side.

Sultana Haydee is pleased; can it be true that her Edmond might finally look on her as she does him – as a lover and soul-mate? She says, "Since you are now my slave, I decree by the powers you have restored to me that this elegant yacht is my floating embassy, and my sovereign territory, and I so order you to ask me for my hand in marriage; and, as my parents are in heaven and you cannot therefore ask Sultan Pasha's favor on Earth, look there and listen if Heaven does not answer in your heart, with a resounding 'Yes, you are indeed a worthy son-in-law.'"

"Still waters run that deep?" Le Comte questions himself. "This woman is truly more mysterious and powerful than I myself was obliged to convince all of Parisian Society. Should I accede to her decree, or feign not to hear what Heaven is truly saying? Should I give my whole heart, soul, mind and body to a woman who will rule me so powerfully and mysteriously? Is it possible that I can trust again?"

Haydee puts her finger on his lips. "Shhh, don't answer yet. Let us first enjoy a dessert made with the love of my heart. I've concocted a sweet invention to satisfy your unique palate."

Le Comte opens his watering mouth as Haydee slowly brings a slice of multi-layered cake to his lips. After tasting the coffee-infused delicacy, both crunchy and smooth, he exclaims, "The most scrumptious dessert on earth. What do you call it?"

"I have named it *tiramisu*," she answers, "after the Italian phrase for 'take me up.' Just as you have taken me up to a level of happiness I have never before experienced, so this dessert recreates that feeling."

Haydee next brings to his lips a warm red liquid. "Oh no," he thinks, "has she believed the rumors that I am that vampire, Lord Ruthwen?" His anxiety calms as he smells nutmeg instead, and tastes a warm, spicy merlot.

"Gluvine," she whispers, naming her invention into his ear.

"Oh siren, you have achieved a subtle chemistry I could not hope to match," declares the Count.

"If that be your verdict, know, sire, that you were the inspiration, the master of my desire. Let my recipes delight your senses, and prepare yourself to behold me return in less formal attire."

Dantes appreciates the beauty of her exquisite frock, as she turns to depart. The moon has slowly risen into the sky as he savored her dessert delights, and its beams shine ethereally through the round starboard window.

Haydee slips into her boudoir, picking up her guitar-like guzla on a whim. The Count is rhapsodized by the sound of her singing, as she strums the strings of her instrument, serenading him to increase his anticipation. Dantes feels hypnotized by the sounds of these mesmerizing words floating from her voice into his ears:

"My lord is my slave

Am I worthy of his praise?

Yet I was his slave

How shall I now behave?"

Meanwhile, the citizens of Paris buzz like busy bees, pollinating and cross-pollinating the rumors of the clamorous events which swirled around that one man, the Count of Monte Cristo. Villefort, the once-upon-a-time crown prosecutor, is now the first patient incarcerated in the Count's newly established insane asylum in Auteuil, named "House de Saint-Meran." Villefort is being rehabilitated, so that he can stand trial for the apparent crime so stealthily exposed by Monte Cristo. Villefort repeatedly begs to be allowed to dig in the back yard, while making the bizarre claim that Edmond Dantes has risen from the grave to avenge him. Yet the Count is oblivious to the fact that his name is on the lips of every member of the Parisian elite and their servants. Haydee's lips preoccupy his thoughts, as he listens to her bewitching music and stares at a pastel by Raphael of nature being colored by autumn.

He can only remember one time in his life that he felt such a state of nirvana, and that had been when he experimented with those green pills of hashish and opium. He wonders if Haydee has drugged him, or if he is merely intoxicated by her love for him. He had realized, upon first using those drugs, that indulging in their potency more than once would lead to a destructive addiction, so he now controls his desire to experience that euphoric sensation and its temporary oblivion.

No, he decides, as he stands to test his equilibrium. He is in full possession of his faculties.

In her boudoir, Haydee drapes a sheer veil over her face and wraps her body in a swath of shimmering cloth, preparing herself to look like the genie in the tale of the *One Thousand and One Nights*. Her future Sultan is entranced by that famous story, and she knows her appearance will tantalize him. She also realizes that it will be hard to break through the Antarctic reserve that has frozen her Sinbad's ability to ravish the woman he is accustomed to protecting; she will have to use more than her charm, beauty and newfound prowess in the arts of seduction. She will have to make him unable to resist her.

"My love," she says, slipping back into the cabin and lighting the coal in her hookah. "Will you partake with me?"

Dantes' eyes light up with delight, as he sees what appears to be a real genie dancing before him. He answers, "My love, you know I never partake."

"Not even for me?" Haydee asks demurely.

Before he can say "No," she inhales deeply from the hookah, then presses her mouth to his and forces the smoke down his lungs.

"Don't exhale," she says. "That is an order from your Sultana."

He holds his breath until he feels dizzy, then intoxicated, by the thrill more than the wine, and he slowly realizes it is not just perfumed smoke he has inhaled – it is cannabis. His body and mind relax instantly.

Haydee takes Dantes' hand, walking him to her bed and laying him down. With the grace of a ballerina, she arches her leg over him and descends upon his hips, beginning to unbutton his shirt.

Her veil still covering her face, Haydee continues to undress her lover.

Perched on his thighs, she runs her hands over his muscular chest and then slowly shrugs her raiment of silk from her shoulders. Her veil remains her only covering, and at last she removes it, too.

For the first time, as Haydee takes Dantes' virgin hands and places them on her bare breasts, he realizes she is voluptuous. "Have you heard of the Kama Sutra?" asks Haydee.

"No. Teach me," requests Dantes, lying through his teeth; as a worldly man, he has of course heard of the famed techniques, even if he has not experienced them. "Share with me all you know."

Haydee presses her mouth onto his and kisses him deeply; his breath began to quicken, and she grows rosy and flushed with passion.

"My lover, you are the first, the last and the only one who shall know my touch," she promises him. "While you were endeavoring to take revenge against mine enemy, I was studying how to reward you."

"My God!" cries Dantes softly, "I have tasted the nectar of the gods."

"No, my lover, my kiss is but a small appetizer. The nectar is reserved for later; first enjoy the main course." Haydee begins to undulate her hips over Dantes' submissive body, in a gentle rhythm that mimics the ebb and flow of the Mediterranean. The pale moonlight, streaming through the starboard window, gleams dazzlingly on her smooth white shoulders.

The night ends in a wonderful catharsis for the newlyweds.

BOOK II COUNT II

CAPTAIN MEDUSALOCKS AND HIS BLACK STYGIAN IBLIS

ON THE THIRD WATCH, DANTES AWAKES IN A **COLD SWEAT.** He is so troubled by the nightmare that he is unable to fall back to sleep, so he eases his arm out from under the sleeping Haydee and slips from the room. Once he is assured she has not heard him leave her side, he moves to the helm and gazes out over the placid ocean, pondering his frightening dream.

Satan had appeared to him, having the hair and forehead of Fernand, the eyes and nose of Danglars, and the mouth and chin of Villefort, but with the fangs of a vampire. Satan's voice combined all three of his traitors' voices as one voice. The eerie sound still echoes in his ears. In the nightmare, Dantes found himself back in prison, digging for his freedom, but instead of meeting prisoner number twenty-seven and seeing Abbe Faria's face, Satan awaited his arrival. Startled, Dantes asked, "Where is Le Abbe?"

"Dead," said the vampire.

"Why are you here?" asked Dantes.

"To prevent your escape!" exclaimed Satan.

Dantes was petrified, even in the haze of the dream. Satan, seeing his victim frozen in fear, slowly moved his fangs toward Dantes' jugular vein. Realizing that he had already escaped from his prison, Dantes regained speech, saying, "Why prevent my escape?"

"I must thwart you from destroying my most productive servants in Paris, and punish you for using my name for your own purposes, and without paying true homage to me."

"How did I use your name?" asked Dantes. He felt his mouth growing dry with fear, and fought to hide the trembling in his limbs.

"When you told Danglars that 'Satan showed you all the kingdoms of the world, as he does all men,' you lied that you had asked 'to be Providence' and then quoted me as saying that I could only 'grant that you be the *right hand* of Providence.' I make such an offer to only my most devoted servants, and I have now brought you back in time to punish you for your insolence and hubris."

Dantes responded, "I said those words only as part of my plan to strike fear into that devil who threw me into years of hellish torment. As for using your name, I didn't believe you existed, so I had no intention of insulting you. You must pardon me."

At that Satan asked, "Have you not read the book of Job, where I made a wager with God that if God withheld His protection, then Job would curse God?"

"Yes, Le Abbe told me to 'apply that story to my life to better understand,' but I only thought of your satanic majesty as an allegorical figure."

"Now that you have used my name in vain, all bets are off. God loses this wager, and your soul belongs to me for eternal torment."

At that, Satan lunged toward Dantes' neck, his fangs growing longer, and Dantes felt the evil creature's breath on his skin, before he jolted awake in the cold sweat that had brought him to the helm.

It had felt so real, but now that Dantes is out in the salty night air, he begins to grow calm. He ponders his past, feeling grateful for the present and wondering what his future will bring. Does he want to become the Sultan of Monte Cristo and, ergo, Sultan of Albania, or should he return to the carefree life of his youthful self and start his life anew with Haydee?

Looking up at the dazzling, star-studded night sky, Dantes realizes that Job didn't take revenge on anyone; and Joseph, who was sold into slavery by ten of his brothers, but whose story Dantes had willfully ignored, still managed to turn the other cheek. Didn't Joseph have as much reason for revenge? Dantes thinks to himself, "Didn't Joseph rise to wealth and power only after, and probably as a result of, his slavery and imprisonment? Am I not a modern Joseph on my way to rule Albania as Sultan? None of this would have been possible without the sad chain of events that first led to my imprisonment, yet was transformed into glory. Perhaps I was the right hand of God in the way I exacted my revenge."

Opening the Bible randomly, Dantes lets his eyes fall to a verse that strikes him with lightning force: "Vengeance is mine, I will repay." Thinking out loud, he questions himself, "Joseph forgave his brothers and blessed them, so why did I not do the same? Who shall I be in this new phase of my life?" Then he remembers the slim volumes Haydee keeps in the room she occupied as a maiden, before she joined him in his bed; he collects them and sits down to read, hoping to find the same solace and wisdom she has possessed.

Dantes is so deeply absorbed in the tome that he almost misses the black hulk on the horizon; it is the most notorious pirate ship in Mediterranean history, the Black Stygian Iblis, whose captain, Medusalocks, causes panic and spreads frenzy in any crew struck, or brave enough to attack. Captain Medusalocks' handle and infamy is partly due to the thick groves of ebony dreadlocks protruding from his head and face, flowing to his chest. Standing seven feet tall and weighing 400 pounds, he has the appearance of a giant. His presence is made all the more fearful by his fierce black eyes and the five-foot sword that hangs off of the leather belt that cinches his thick black robes.

Though Dantes is normally prepared for any adventure, even he is reluctant and ill-equipped to defeat an adversary so terrifying.

Dantes is a man of infinite resources, however, and there are few situations from which he cannot artfully extricate himself. During an expedition to the Amazon, he had learned the art of paralyzing or killing his enemies with poisonous darts. He had brought the materials back, as well as the memories, and he knows now why he had felt compelled to do so – there is always an occasion for every skill learned. Dantes calls Ali, his mute Nubian slave, to prepare to use his collection of deadly darts in the upcoming clash with the nefarious captain.

"Ali, do you remember how to use these blow darts?" Dantes asks, running his fingers over the shiny, slim bits of wood as they rest in their plush case.

Ali indicates "Yes," by stuffing an imaginary dart into an imaginary mouthpiece and imitating a blow.

"Very good," says Dantes. "When Haydee shows herself on deck and distracts the Gorgonic giant with her beauty, I will somehow draw Medusalocks to our ship. Once I have done so, aim for his neck as I lunge at him with my sword. Use the paralyzing dart. If I am defeated, use the poisonous darts. Hide where you can't be seen, killing each pirate as he attempts to row or swim to our vessel. I will inform the rest of the crew to set sail for Albania, should I fall.

"If the worst happens, and I am among you no longer, then use these papers, carry out re-establishing the Pasha Sultanate, and install Haydee as Sultana." Ali nods his head, tears welling up in his eyes. Though he cannot express his thoughts in words, he takes Dantes' hand in a strong shake, reaffirming their bond.

Before the Black Iblis draws near enough to make its demands of surrender, Dantes disguises himself as an Imam and preemptively yells out to the crew of the Black Iblis, "Tell your cowardly captain that Sultan Sinbad Zahfan al Jihad Ghaffar bin Taqwa din Nushur Buri al Mahdee demands a duel on the deck of his yacht. Winner takes all. Your prize, although your hopes of winning are pathetically slim, will be this yacht and its treasures, including the genie from the tales of the *One Thousand and One Nights.*

"If you lose, however, the magnificent Sultan Sinbad will become the commander-in-chief, adding the Black Iblis and its crew of criminals to his Albanian war-fleet.

"If your captain is not a coward, he will accept this challenge and be on our deck in one hour with the weapon of his choice; and Sultan Sinbad will be prepared, ready to use the same weapon, whether it is sword, pistol, or dagger. Your captain has five minutes to confirm his choice of weapon."

The pirates of the Iblis crew erupt into hysterical laughter with this strange pronouncement, and their merriment lasts until the fearsome captain emerges drunk, demanding, "Who is this Sultan Sinbad who wants to give me his life, yacht, and treasures?"

Dantes goes below and quickly removes his first disguise, replacing it with a woven wig of black dreadlocks and a set of obsidian robes, designed to hide the stilts that make him appear seven and a half feet tall.

As Dantes emerges taller than Captain Medusalocks, the Iblis crew gasps.

"So, coward, will it be sword, pistol or dagger?" shouts Dantes.

Captain Medusalocks looks at his crew, realizing if he declines the duel, he will indeed be seen as a coward. Apprehensively he shouts back, "I will bring my sword, but why have I never heard of you before on the wild seas?"

"I am the hand of divine Providence. Allah the Great raised me up in order to defeat Satan, and to subdue your jinns to His will. Allah showed you to me in my dream last night, as the phantom of Satan. Your skull will become my navy's masthead to terrify any who dare attack my fleet."

After that brash speech, Dantes goes back down below the deck, leaving Medusalocks scratching his head. Haydee, who has been awakened by the noise, is now awaiting him to ask what is happening above deck. She pulls her robes tightly over her young, lithe body. Trembling, she asks, "What have you done?"

"My love," Dantes explains quickly, "if I had not shown my own courage in challenging the dreaded Captain Medusalocks to a duel, the Iblis would by now be pillaging our ship. Fighting them would have been futile – they are too mighty in number and much too fierce in warcraft. But have faith, my sweet Sultana; the name I have given them is the key to our future together as rulers of Albania. 'Zahfan' means battle plan, which we just made; 'Jihad' means holy war, which we just declared; 'Ghaffar' means 'Forgiver,' which I want to learn to be; 'Taqwa' means fear of Allah; which I wish to instill; 'din' means justice, which I intend to execute; 'Nushur' means resurrection, due to my death as Dantes; 'Buri' means liberator, as I intend to liberate your people with your blessing; 'al Mahdee' sums up these names."

Haydee interjects, "But my Liberator, what inspired this? Our vessel is swift – surely we could have just fled to safety."

Dantes answers, "You confessed that you are a Muslim, just before you slept last night; so, unable to sleep myself after a terrible nightmare, I studied the Koran to make myself your worthy servant, husband

and Sultan of Albania. The text of that holy book has inspired me to be brave and worthy of you, as well as to gain glory in Allah's eyes."

"Allah has answered my prayers," Haydee says. "Do you love me enough to defeat that monster?"

"With the taste of Eden still on my lips, I am not ready to die. Far beyond that, my greatest purpose is to protect you and to keep you happy. I will not accept death as the outcome of this battle."

"If you fail, I will throw myself overboard, so that I can join you in paradise," Haydee says.

"My love," says Dantes, "though I seem dead, don't believe. Remember, Dantes died, as did Valentine; but death did not yet give its final sting. Always have hope and wait for me. Promise me that."

"This is too much to promise, if I believe you dead. I have just found happiness in your arms – I cannot bear to be separated from them in this life." Her voice is filled with emotion, and Dantes's heart swells in return; he knows he has finally found the woman he dreamed of, one who will eternally be loyal and true.

Knowing that Haydee's life is determined by the success of the upcoming duel, Dantes prays, "God of Heaven, give me the strength to protect Haydee and deliver Medusalocks subdued into my hands." He then hefts his sickle-shaped, lightweight sword and returns to the deck to face the infamous Mediterranean pirate, Captain Medusalocks.

Medusalocks charges immediately, but Dantes dodges the first attack easily; the additional height granted him by the stilts make striding across the wooden slats of the deck effortless. As he ducks behind the helm, he throws his voice across the deck, making it sound as if anguished screams and the hissing of a hundred snakes is coming from Medusalocks's beard. The jinnish pirates stop their jeering in shock, and Medusalocks pauses and looks down, seeking the source of the noise. Taking advantage of the distraction and darting forward, Dantes cuts off half of Medusalocks' beard and throws it in the air with a yell of victory.

Recovering quickly and slamming his long sword into Dantes' thigh, Captain Medusalocks recoils when he realizes he hasn't cut living flesh. "Who is this Sultan Sinbad?" he mutters to himself. "A creature of myth?" But upon regaining his courage, Medusalocks strikes Sinbad's thigh once again. Dantes feels his stilt crack and stumbles back, trying to regain his balance.

Haydee enters the scene in her genie attire, veiled and swathed in silk, strumming and singing the same song she had composed and sung to Dantes, before they had both been consumed with lust. Her appearance distracts the Gorgonic pirate just as Dantes had predicted, giving the Count time to recover and thrust his sword toward the giant's chest. Ali aims true at the perfect moment, and the blow dart strikes in the same instant that Dantes' blade leaves a thin slice across Medusalocks's chest. The giant reaches for his neck and moments later crumples to the ground.

Both the crew of jinns and the crew of the yacht cry out with joy, singing:

"We give thanks to Allah the Greatest
For sending us Sinbad the Bravest
Triumphant is our liberator by Justice
Because he defeated Satan's Injustice"

According to Greek lore, blood extracted from a Gorgon can be used to raise the dead and kill; so Sinbad bleeds two vials from the giant pirate, who is rumored to be an actual member of the ancient family of Gorgons. Dantes knows he can use that rumor and Medusalocks' blood in the future to play on the crew's superstitions. Dantes puts the vials of blood on dry ice, one of his recent inventions.

As the effects of the tranquilizer begin to wear off, Dantes places his foot on Captain Medusalocks's chest and presses the point of his sword to the pirate's throat.

His men quickly tie the giant's hands and, with great effort, move him into the brig of the Iblis, where four pirates are stationed to guard him in shifts night and day.

BOOK II COUNT III

ADMIRAL JARRE OF THE FRENCH NAVY

EXHILARATED BY COMMANDEERING THE GARGANTUAN IBLIS, DANTES realizes what he should have felt when he had first taken command as captain of the Pharaon. He feels a renewed sense of freedom, which brings back his youthful spirit of adventure. He wonders if he should live the life of a pirate, sailing around the world like an itinerant god, instead of being tied down as the Sultan of Albania.

As Dantes considers his options, the Zephyrus west-wind of the Mediterranean is giving off her refreshing salty, aromatic spray. Her waters turn magically from amethyst to hot azure to hazy purple at sunset, giving Dantes the inspiration to turn the Iblis into a small, though luxurious, floating city.

Dantes turns to his new crew of pirates and says, "Do I have your loyalty?"

"Yes!" shout the ruffians; Medusalocks had been a cruel master, and already they can see that Dantes treats his own crew with kindness and respect.

"Then you must take the following oath: 'We, the crew of the Black Stygian Iblis, swear to Allah and on our reputation to protect, obey, and honor the majestic Sultana Haydee and her slave, Sultan Sinbad al Mahdee; and to follow all of their commands, edicts and orders faithfully, obediently and expeditiously."

"Yeah!" each says in unison, as they repeat the oath verbatim, adding, "And we shall sacrifice our lives freely, if needed."

Dantes' first order is to prepare for a great feast. Haydee teaches the cooks new techniques for presenting a feast fit for Sultans. The sailors, still reveling in their freedom, spontaneously sing songs of liberation and gratitude, with joy and delight, all day and late into the night.

Satisfied with an enormous feast of fresh-fried whitefish, pita bread, and hummus, Dantes appoints a few members of his crew to watch the horizon, and returns to his bedchamber for more of Haydee's charms. When they finally fall asleep, exhausted after the events of the day, they remain wrapped in one another's arms, their hearts filled with peace and contentment.

Dantes awakens the next morning to a loud voice shouting in French, "You are surrounded by the French Navy. Surrender and save your lives!"

Dantes has suspected that a stronger naval fleet would attempt to capture what had for so long been a feared pirate vessel, but as always, he is prepared. Hurriedly arising from bed, Dantes dons his most pretentious admiral's uniform, one he had designed for just such an occasion, with large gold braids flowing off its shoulders. He goes on deck and responds in an Albanian accent that he copies from Haydee's own, "I, Sultan Sinbad Zahfan al Jihad Ghaffar bin Taqwa din Nushur Buri al Mahdee, admiral and sovereign of the Sultanate of Albania, propose a treaty with the navy of France.

"We have defeated the infamous pirate, Captain Medusalocks, and will deliver his satanic majesty to your custody today, as a token of our friendship. Our ships will aid France, when called upon, as a part of this proposed treaty."

Dantes, hearing no reply, continues, "I await your presence on my master's yacht, the Majestic Haydee's Wanderlust, for inspection and the signing ceremony."

Admiral Alexandre Jarre, commander of the French navy, replies, "How can we know this is not a trick of the devil Captain Medusalocks? We have been fooled by him before."

"Monsieur Admiral Jarre, recall the reputation of the Iblis and use your common sense. We will send you the Gorgonic captain in advance of further negotiations, as a good faith gesture, on your word that such goodwill shall cease your hostility toward us."

"So agreed!" shouts Admiral Jarre. "We are ready to receive the vanquished pirate."

It humbles the French navy to see that a small crew of men could capture a pirate their own country had chased for decades, and upon conferring for a few minutes, they agree to sign the treaty. On board the luxurious "Majestic Haydee's Wanderlust," the Sultan and the Admiral set their hands and seals to the extraordinary treatise, subject to ratification by Paris' Minister of Foreign Affairs.

The men celebrate their newfound alliance by indulging in two glasses of sweet port, and slices of Haydee's delicious tiramisu.

"What a delightful dessert," Admiral Monsieur Jarre says. "How is it made?"

Sultan Sinbad says, "That is a secret of Her Majesty, Sultana Haydee. Even I, her slave and first man, find it to be a mystery. And if Haydee has her way, it will be centuries yet before the secret is revealed."

"I shall be delighted to have the honor of spreading the good news of your capture of the terrible Iblis pirate, making you the most famous and glorious foreigner in the mind of Parisian society," Admiral Jarre says. "I also will arrange for your royal and diplomatic arrival to visit our head of state, at which time you will be received and accorded the highest honors, pomp and ceremony, sparing no cost." Admiral Jarre is oblivious to the fact that Admiral Sinbad is already the most famous person in France, under the title "Count of Monte Cristo."

After exchanging flowery words of friendship, Dantes jests in a serious tone of voice, "Always keep the Gorgon's deadly dreadlocks trimmed."

When the French ship has sailed, Dantes returns to Haydee and gathers her into his arms. "My love, you have proven a magnificent partner," he whispers into her ear. He blushes with shame, when he realizes he has almost called her Mercedes; thoughts of returning to Paris have also stirred in his breast old emotions about his first love.

As he pulls back from his new wife, he smiles to hide his guilt and says, "I have a surprise for you, my darling." From the captain's desk at which he writes his daily logs, Dantes pulls forth an elaborately decorated set of documents demonstrating proof of their marriage, documents that have been signed and sealed by his in-house Arabian Imam. Haydee is delighted by this creativity and claps her hands in a girlish display of glee. "We are officially married!" she cries, studying the documents and then clasping them to her heart.

Pointing toward the south, Dantes says, "I have still more for you, Sultana. Behold, on that yonder island, Lampedusa, Arabian horses from my stable await us for hunting pheasant with my falcons. This is for our honeymoon, a gift that my heart hopes will delight you."

Haydee's face lights up, and she says gleefully, "You are my heart. What your heart hopes makes my heart's dream come true."

When the ship draws as close at it can to Lampedusa, Dantes has Ali lower him and his bride down to the sea in a small rowboat, and Dantes proceeds to row his love to shore. On the desert island of the Mediterranean, Dantes introduces Haydee to Wajh, a falcon trained by the Maltese, and to Sabr, a falcon he himself trained in Arabia.

"Sabr is all yours," Dantes says. "Command her as you desire, but first talk to her so she knows your voice, and observe how I handle Wajh. Both of these beautiful falcons' names were inspired by the Koran, 'Wajh' meaning countenance, and 'Sabr,' meaning steadfastness."

Their falcons catch four quail and one pheasant. The newlyweds roast two of the game birds on an open fire, leaving two raw quail for Wajh and Sabr. Haydee and Dantes eventually fall asleep on the sand, after a romantic evening.

BOOK II COUNT IV

MERCEDES' DISCOVERY

MEANWHILE, THOUGH SHE IS NOW FAR FROM DANTES' MIND, MERCEDES MAKES an intriguing discovery. She finds a hiding place where Dantes' father, Louis, had secreted a letter. She cannot believe her eyes as she reads:

"The Year of our Lord, July 16, 1815

"Edmond, my dear Son,

"I wanted to tell you in person, but my dreams last night revealed that my death will precede your return. You may have noticed, by the time you receive this unbelievable missive, that you have a very unique destiny. You may have also forgotten the bedtime stories your mother, Virginia Magdalene, told you before she passed on when you were seven. You probably thought those were only fairy tales, if you do remember them at all. The stories were actually the history of your mother's family, dating back to the time of Christ Jesus. I myself did not realize until after her death that the stories were not fiction. With this message, you will find my research and the family trees of the Merovingian Dynasty, as well as of the Royal House of David – both parts of your mother's family tree. Your direct line from the Frankish kings is not what amazed me so much; rather, what has unnerved me so completely is that the same Mary Magdalene from the Bible arrived right here on the beaches of Marseilles. Growing up, we were raised on the legend of Magdalene's arrival. When I met your mother, I half seriously asked if she was related. At first, I thought she was joking when she casually said, 'Yes.' Not thinking that was anything to be proud of, due to the Catholic Church falsely painting her as a prostitute, I asked who your mother's forefather was. She replied, 'That is the gravest of mysteries, a family secret. If I tell you, I'll have to become a black widow.' I realized this was a dark secret, assuming she might not even know her forefather's identity, in light of Mary Magdalene's so-called history of prostitution. I didn't push further, because I realized it could be an embarrassing revelation.

"After your mother's passing, I had some strange visits from men claiming to belong to various orders of knighthood, such as Malta, Templar and Melchizedek, claiming that they were charged with protecting you, but I assured them I would take good care of you.

"Your mother didn't realize that I sometimes overheard the strange stories she repeated to you on stormy nights. On her deathbed, she requested that when you reached twenty-one years of age, you would be told, quote, 'the stories that captivated you as a child were not fairy tales, but my family's real histories. Your forefather was, and is, the greatest central figure in history,' unquote. I leave you this truth with my blessing, as your sole legacy. You will face what seem to be insurmountable obstacles in life, yet be of good cheer, and take to heart these words, 'He who overcomes and continues in my (your forefather's) works will I give power over the nations; and he shall rule them, even as I overcame and am set at the right hand of my father, God.' This verse may also inspire you: 'Thou art a priest forever, after the order of Melchizedec, the king of peace and righteousness.'

"Your mother also said, and this was most mysterious to me, 'If you are unable to resurrect from antiquity the Ancient Royal House of David, fear not, you will help pave the way; and if not you, one of your offspring or relatives from my family will do so, as the Branch of David.'

"Edmond, your dear mother went on to tell me that she only lived for you. I can tell you that I only lived for her and for you; and now that we will not see each other again in this world, there is no reason for me to linger; so I will now say farewell, my true and dearest Son. Be strong to the end, as your mother and I will be waiting to welcome you on the other side with a warm embrace.

"Yours faithfully and devotedly,
Papa"

Mercedes reads the strange letter several times in the weeks after she discovers it, and it awakens in her feelings she had thought were dead. Though she has long struggled to push romantic thoughts of Edmond Dantes from her mind, the letter reminds her what an amazing man he truly is – more amazing, apparently, than even she has ever realized. Now that she has started her life over, the feelings of possibility and youth have returned to her. Life seems vibrant. Spinning hemp, the pastime which occupies some of her daylight hours, brings back thoughts and feelings of the days of her youth when she was singularly in love with Edmond. The eerie missive rekindles that fire that was smoldering, nearly extinguished, like an old dream that could hardly be recalled, coming back to life.

Mercedes notices her reflection in the mirror, as she walks back to her spindle. Is she imaging a bright twinkle in her eyes? Does the hemp-oil tincture she concocted really make her skin look smooth and supple? One day, as she walks along the sunny beaches of Marseilles, she notices her skin has regained its glow and her body is toned with golden hues; but is that the only reason she appears so young and stunningly beautiful as she admires her reflection in the mirror the following afternoon? "No," she reflects. "A curse has been lifted from me. I'm still in my forties, but can my true love forgive me? Is it too late? Has he found another? It seems he wants me as a part of his life, to place me in Marseilles, in his father's apartment, to flood my mind with our past together. I don't think his purpose is to punish me, since I am slowly healing."

Her hopes that Dantes might one day return to her gives Mercedes new ambition. Part of her time was spent studying a large collection of chemistry and botanical books found in pere Dantes library. Experimenting with the various properties of the hemp plant, Mercedes is the first to produce soap, milk, and cheese made of its seeds. She also notices the skin lotion she has created gives off a lovely fragrance. "Why not make a business out of this?" she thinks. "I cannot live off of Edmond's generosity forever, and perhaps if he sees I am a woman who can take care of herself, an independent lady, he may love me again."

Mercedes sets out for Monsieur Maximillien Morrel's little house on the Rue Meslay, but she only finds his sister Julie and Julie's husband, Emmanuel, at home working in their small garden. As Mercedes approaches, Emmanuel says, "Look, Julie, Countess Madame Morcerf has graced us with her presence. What have we done to deserve this honor?"

"Please, Monsieur, I no longer wish to be addressed as 'Countess,' and my son, Albert, and I have restored my maiden name, Herrera. Please call me Mercedes," Mercedes says, having heard the title Emmanuel bestowed upon her.

"Very well. Greetings, Mercedes. We are pleased to receive you. We've heard nothing but good spoken of you and your noble son, Albert," says Julie. "Please come inside, and we will offer you what we have."

Over Turkish coffee and hamantasch pastries infused with poppy seeds and cherries, Mercedes enthusiastically relays how she has developed oil, soap, milk and cheese from hemp seeds, offering her hosts samples as evidence.

"Do you think there will be a demand for these products?" asks Mercedes. "I am eager to hear what you think of them, but I must admit, I came here with other motives. I wish to find the man who has been most important to me and has, indeed, saved me from poverty and a life of shame. Can you assist me in getting a message to the Count of Monte Cristo, as I realize that Maximillien is a close friend?"

Julie says, "The Count of Monte Cristo is our best friend and our cherished savior, as well. Please give us the message and we will relay it to him."

Mercedes replies, "Kindly inform Monsieur Le Comte that Mercedes Herrera requests an audience with his Excellency to reveal his father, Louis Dantes' last words. I wish to deliver the letter in person, either in Monsieur Dantes' old apartment or here. Though, if need be, I will travel to the ends of the earth to deliver the missive personally, wherever that mysterious man may reside."

"We will do what we can to make sure Monsieur Le Comte gets the message as quickly as possible," Julie promises. "I'm sure he will be eager to hear his father's final message."

As she guides Mercedes through the garden and to the gate, Mercedes comments, "Your garden is lovely – so filled with beauty and color."

"You may plant your hemp seeds here, if you like," says Emmanuel. "We have two hectare in the backyard, and I would be pleased to take over the planting and harvesting on your behalf."

"Would you?" Mercedes replies. "I've been hoping to expand, and take my products perhaps even to Paris. Shall we make it a partnership?"

"It is settled!" declares Julie. "Let us shake hands to seal our oath."

The three shake hands, then spontaneously hug, realizing their common bond in the Count of Monte Cristo.

BOOK II COUNT V

HOUSE OF AUTEUIL

THE SULTAN OF MONTE CRISTO FINDS HIMSELF **STRUGGLING** to reconcile the differences between the Holy Bible and the Holy Koran.

He notices there is agreement on Christ Jesus being "the messiah born of a virgin," but he is concerned that the Bible has been retold in a way to create a revised bible and religion that elevates Mohammed and his subjects above the more authentic and ancient holy writ. He is struck by the Koran's depiction of God as most merciful, oft forging, patient, and full of loving-kindness. In the Old Testament of the Bible that Dantes was raised upon, God was a vengeful and angry entity. He begins to wonder which is the true God, or if they are aspects of the same. Can he embrace both religions?

Regardless of his struggles with accepting which is the true god, Dantes finds edicts commanding forgiveness of others' wrongs in both texts and, after consultation with Haydee, decides it is time to forgive Villefort. He prepares for his journey to 28 Rue de la Fontaine, the House of Auteuil, where Villefort is being rehabilitated. Dantes spends the journey to Paris poring over the Bible and the Koran, making notes and charts on the texts to pass the time. When he reaches Paris once more, the smells, sights, and sounds of the city assault him – he has thought he was ready to move on and forgive those who wronged him, but now he is not so sure.

Unsure if Villefort will recognize him, Dantes disguises himself as a doctor, darkening his face and donning a curly white wig. The Sultan of Monte Cristo enters patient room number one, after being let in by his faithful servant, Monsieur Bertuccio. Villefort is at a battered desk, scribbling frantically. Looking up at his visitor, he asks, "Who let you in? Can't you see I am preparing an indictment and am not to be disturbed?"

"I am sorry to disturb you, Excellency," Dantes says smoothly. "My name is Dr. Maurice Adelmonte. May I ask whom the crown prosecutor has named as the defendant?"

"Myself," Villefort responds.

"What are the crimes brought against you?"

"My first crime was to send an innocent man to prison for life; and his ghosts have risen to haunt me. My second and most hideous crime was to bury my newly-born son alive in the garden downstairs; his ghost grew into a young man to haunt me at trial. I dig every day in that cursed garden, but I cannot find his remains. My crimes beyond that are more than I can count – they have been of both soul and body," concludes Villefort.

"As your doctor, Monsieur Le Comte," says Dr. Adelmonte, "it is my responsibility to restore your mental health, so that you can stand trial. Otherwise, you will spend the rest of your life digging up the garden in the courtyard and scribbling out your crimes in these imaginary indictments. Do I have your attention? Will you let me help you?"

Edmond Dantes fights off the pleasure running through his veins – to be in a position of so much power over the man who had destroyed his youth and happiness. He plays with the idea of making Villefort's life even more miserable, as he awaits his former enemy's answer. Villefort breaks down in tears, his sobs so raw that they touch Dantes' heart. Seeing that the man both needs and wants help, Dantes goes on to say, "Monsieur, I think the best way to restore your health is to tell you the truth – to shed light into the dark corners of your mind.

"As to your crime against Edmond Dantes, I can assure you that he has forgiven you and that he did not rise from the dead as a specter. Instead, he accidently faked his death when he escaped from his dungeon on Chateau D'If. That is a very long story; but you can read the entire account in the biography entitled *The Count of Monte Cristo,* by investigative reporter Alexandre Dumas. Here, take the book about him and read it before my next visit in a fortnight – it will set your mind at ease, I do believe.

"You need not dig anymore in the garden, because the illegitimate son you sired with the baroness Danglars did not die, as you thought. In fact, a Corsican, Monsieur Bertuccio, was hiding in the shadows and waiting to take his revenge against you for your refusal to seek justice against those who murdered his brother. He witnessed you bury the baby, thinking it only a bundle, and then stabbed you, thinking he killed you. He dug up what he expected to be buried treasure; but instead, he found an umbilically-strangled infant, who began to move as he was held in the Corsican's warm arms.

"Monsieur Bertuccio saved the baby's life. So, that was not your son's grown ghost you indicted and faced at trial, but your lost-and-found son who had merely been raised by another. Read Chapter XLIV, entitled 'The Vendetta,' to completely refresh your memory and learn the details.

"Before you read the book I have given you, take this medicine I have brought you. It will calm you and help you sort out these facts. Don't ask for it again, however – it is a dangerous and strong drug, and many men have fallen prey to its hold. You would be no different, and I will not have your life wasted. After you have taken the medicine and read the book, your mind should be healed. I will arrange for Baroness Danglars to see you to help with your recovery."

Villefort seems to have been hypnotized by these revelations, making no sound as Dantes speaks, and obediently takes the dosage of hashish and morphine. A cloud of puzzled doubt forms on his face. "I seem to remember Madame Heloise Villefort speak of you as a great doctor. Did you not meet her in Italia?"

"Yes indeed, I did have the delightful pleasure of making the acquaintance of your lovely, dearly-departed wife," Dantes says, smiling at the memory. "It was in Perugia, on the day of Corpus Christi, in the garden of hostery of the Post, that chance brought us together; your wife, your daughter Mademoiselle Valentine, and your dearly departed son, Édouard. It was on a burning hot day and your family was waiting for some horses that were delayed in arriving, because of the festival. Your wife was sitting on a stone bench under the arbor, while Édouard chased a peacock, happily extracting three long, beautiful feathers from its tail. I recall that Mademoiselle Valentine needed Neapolitan air to benefit her lungs, according to your family doctor's suggestions.

"We spoke for a long time, Monsieur, of various things: of Perugino, of Raphael, of the manners and customs of the place, and about the celebrated aqua tofana, the secret of which, I believe, Madame had been told was still kept by some people in Perugia.

"Madame de Villefort was keenly interested in the good health of your daughter, and consulted with me for her benefit."

"So why," asks Villefort, "did she poison the helpless girl?"

"This evil idea was planted in her mind by a very skilled and determined Machiavelli," replies Dantes. "Yet I have some good news for you: that same Machiavelli saved her life."

"But, how?!" Villefort cries. "I interred her myself in our family mausoleum in the Pere Lachaise Cemetery, and I recall reciting the elegiac Poem written by Francois de Malherbe to memorialize the death of du Perier's daughter."

"The poison was replaced by powerful drugs that put Valentine in a deep sleep, making her appear dead," says Dantes.

"Who is this Machiavelli that planted the diabolical seed, then uprooted it," asks Villefort, "and how can you know?"

"Ah," says Dantes. "Before I studied medicine, I received the ecclesiastical title of 'Abbe.' Since I received this information under confessional sanctity, I must not divulge the Machiavelli's real name; yet, I am permitted to say that you were the intended target of the vengeful plot. When the Machiavelli realized the beautiful, chaste, sweet young woman, his next victim, was coincidentally the love of his good friend, Maximillien Morrel, the Machiavelli was compelled to intervene."

"But how did he reach her to exchange the fatal dose?" asks Villefort.

"Your Machiavelli's arms reach far and wide," says Dantes, "yet, in this case, he rented your neighbor's property and stealthily entered your home, remaining vigilantly awake for three days, hiding behind the bookcase to replace each tainted lemonade. Your brilliant father,

Noirtier de Villefort, realized the pending danger after the deaths of Valentine's grandparents, Monsieur and Madame de Saint-Meran, and immunized her by having her swallow minute doses of his own poisonous medicine, doubling some every day, also helping to save his precious angel.

"The good news is that two of the children you thought lost are now alive and well, one living in marital bliss and caring for your father, while the other is in a hell, called prison, needing your expert help and the father he never had. I think we can make a good case for his defense – extenuating circumstances. These two surviving children should give you great motivation to recover your mental faculties."

"Yes," says Villefort, "motivation indeed. Yet I find it hard to believe, without seeing and holding my dear daughter, Valentine, in my arms and hearing her voice."

"This will be arranged," Dantes says, "so please rest assured, and when you awake from the purgative dream you will now experience, focus on saving your son, Andrea; and pray with me for the salvation of your dearly departed wife and son, Édouard.

"Thank you, Abbe," says Villefort, "I thank you from the bottom of my once-empty, yet now full heart."

After the nurses tuck Villefort into bed, he begins to think that Dr. Adelmonte reminds him of someone he has met before, but he can't quite place the face or the voice.

Dantes heads out on horseback to meet Julie and Emmanuel at the theater in Paris. He feels carefree, as the spring air blows his hair back.

BOOK II COUNT VI

COUNTESS G

WHEN THE COUNT OF MONTE CRISTO ENTERS HIS coveted spot in the most prestigious Parisian theater, he is overwhelmed by the warm hugs that await him. As Emmanuel and Julie calm, Edmond Dantes notices Mercedes seated, quietly hiding behind her veil. Apprehensively, Edmond takes Mercedes' hand, gently presses his lips to her golden skin, saying, "Mademoiselle Herrera, finding you here has brought me great joy, and fulfilled a hope I had that we would meet again. When I last saw you, you fled from me, and I have felt empty ever since. Have you forgiven me? Have you forgiven yourself?"

Mercedes lifts her eyes to meet his, her gaze concealed by the veil. "Yes Edmond, I have forgiven myself – and as for you, there is nothing to forgive. Letting go of the past has rejuvenated my youthfulness and restored my zeal for life. Lift my veil and tell me if I am dreaming."

Lifting the veil to behold a Mercedes more beautiful than the young bride he once dreamed of marrying, more intoxicating and radiant than Juno, the Queen of Heaven, Edmond says, "You are one of those rare women who grow more beautiful with age."

Mercedes, veiling herself once more, says, "I hope you will not let what you have beheld pine away, without knowing your love. When we are alone again, I have many blessings to shower on you. Will you visit me in your father's apartment tomorrow?"

"Yes, Mercedes, I promise I shall."

Across the theater, the gorgeous Countess G is the first to spot the Count of Monte Cristo, and asks Franz to request Le Comte to visit her between Act I and Act II of "Zarzuela," a comic Spanish opera based on the royal residence near Madrid, first performed in 1770. The Count dutifully does as he is bade, kissing the Countess' hand as he greets her. After formalities are exchanged, she makes her request. "My dear Count, I beg you to visit my chateau tonight, for a soiree. I promise you will never forget it. I will introduce you to that bloodhound of investigative journalism, Alexandre Dumas. He publishes a chapter every day in the Debats about you, and perhaps you know he has published a book about your exploits."

"Indeed," says Dantes, "I have heard rumors and read some of the details in the Debats and the Presse newspapers. He makes me out to be quite an extraordinary, and even frightening, man."

"Frightening," Countess G retorts with a coy smile. "To be frightening, we would need some evidence that you imbibe blood – the only elixir which could stop you from aging. I still believe you are Lord Ruthwen, because no one born in the 1700s could look to be so young."

The Count of Monte Cristo grins, "Would you like me to share my secret nostrum?"

Countess G says, "I will give you my answer this night, but only if you visit my new chateau."

"You can depend on my descent into your little Versailles tonight, dear Countess," Dantes says, as he takes his leave, slowly bowing. "Now, please excuse me – I must return to my seat for the second act."

"Franz!" says Countess G to her companion, as the lights dim. "Did he say 'descent'? Did he mean he would be lowering himself to visit me?"

"I am sure he would not be so insulting," Franz replies. "I think he was playing with your jokes about him being a vampire; that like a bat he would descend from the air to relieve you of your blood. That is what you are hoping, I suspect."

Countess G, blushing, says, "I admit that this vampire, Lord Ruthwen, or whatever he is, has spellbound me; and he has something I want and need. I don't know if this desire is wholesome or diabolical, but I know I must have what I crave or else die."

By this time, all eyes are on the notorious Count of Monte Cristo, and his name is heard on every lip.

Mercedes, observing the interactions between Countess G and the Count of Monte Cristo, clutches her envious heart. Could Dantes be drawn to another?

The Count of Monte Cristo does indeed descend upon the chateau of the wealthy Italian heiress; he brings with him Mercedes, Julie, Emmanuel, and a host of hired servants in a caravan of his phaeton, brougham, coupe, barouche, and britzka carriages, all drawn by the world's finest Arabian horses. As he leads Mercedes in on his arm, he feels a slight twinge of guilt – what would Haydee think of this reunion with his first love? He brushes his misgivings aside, however, telling himself that his intentions are honorable and Mercedes is an old friend, albeit a beautiful one.

As Mercedes watches the finely-dressed couples sweeping across the marble floor of the ballroom, she feels a longing in her own feet to join the elegant movement and tear off the veil she still wears. But her longing goes deeper than that – she longs to have a certain man dance with her, holding her in his strong arms.

Mercedes and Dantes have danced together only a few times in their lives, and their last waltz was twenty years ago. Mercedes quietly asks Dantes to dance with her, hardly daring to hope he will agree. Apprehensively, he accepts, and is surprised to realize that their feet move in rhythmic harmony, as they effortlessly join the graceful flow of Parisian aristocracy. When the orchestra finishes performing Amadeus Mozart's 'Waltz in G Minor,' the women of Parisian high society surround the Count of Monte Cristo, requesting a dance for themselves. They have been watching him and whispering ever since he stepped into the chateau, and now they each want their own turn in his arms. Countess G cuts through her guests and aggressively takes the Count's hand, walking him back to the ballroom floor, as the orchestra begins yet another waltz. Although his chemistry with Countess G is not as engaging as with Mercedes, he still finds her an enjoyable partner. Countess G whispers in his ear, "I have something I want to show you," and takes Dantes' hand, while leading him up along the balustrade of the winding stairs.

Mercedes is outraged as she observes this blatant seduction in front of Paris' aristocratic society. She's not sure if she's more angry at Dantes or at Countess G, but she begins to shake with rage, as the two disappear into the gloom of the upper level.

Countess G leads Dantes into her fashionable bedroom, which contains some of the world's greatest artwork. One piece in particular catches Dantes' eye, but as he moves to inspect it more closely, she pulls him back to the center of the room, laughing. "Don't look at those, my dear Count; look at me," she says, flirtatiously pulling away the scarf that covered her neck. "Look at this tender white, soft skin. Gaze at these blue, virgin veins. I want to be young forever. Please, I beg of you." She gently places his hand on the left side of her neck. "Tenderly avail yourself of my precious blood to satisfy your thirst, and grant me eternal life."

The Count of Monte Cristo, ever amused by the folly of others, cannot help himself – he slowly moves his mouth to her neck, and sucks until she faints. He guides her unconscious body onto the silken linens of her bed, and pulls shut the purple velvet curtains, embroidered with clusters of laburnum and pink acacia branches, so that she is entirely enclosed within.

As he prepares to return to the party, Dantes hears a knock on the door, and finds Ali, who points downstairs, his features indicating that the matter is urgent. "Yes, my good man?" asks Dantes. "Lead and I will follow – show me the source of your distress."

Ali leads Dantes down a back staircase, into a small library off of the ballroom. Mercedes sits inside, on a low ottoman; she has removed her veil and twists it in her hands, and tears streak her cheeks.

Relieved that Dantes has returned with Ali, she asks, "What business do you have with that temptress?"

"Would you be jealous if I added her to my seraglio?" inquires Dantes, laughter in his eyes.

"What is a seraglio?" asks Mercedes, distracted from her pique by Dantes' question.

"A harem palace, my love," Dantes answers. "To live with the rest of my beautiful wives."

"What? You mean to say that you already have a harem of wives?" Mercedes' voice rose in disbelief. "I have never heard of a Westerner of the civilized world engaging in such barbarism."

"How do you know it is barbaric, if you have never tried it?" Dantes asked, his tone turning serious and contemplative. "Haydee has told me many stories of her father's harem. Her mother was his Vasiliki, and she and the other wives treated each other like sisters, and all of the children treated each other like whole, not half, sisters and brothers. It was a large and joyous family of the kind never seen in Europe. And yet Haydee's mother was born a civilized Christian, and she willingly married a Sultan, a Muslim. You respect King Solomon, don't you? Recall he had 700 wives and 300 concubines, authored Proverbs, and built the Lord's temple as well."

"I am not sure I can condone such a life," says Mercedes. "But your revelation reminds me of one of the secrets I have to reveal to you," Mercedes says. "Your father wrote a letter, which he hid before his death, that claims King Solomon in your genealogy; and you won't believe the letter when you read it. If that is your heritage, and you are descended from King Solomon, then having a harem may indeed be your birthright. How did you come to possess a harem, and how many wives have you already wed?"

"As you may know," Dantes answers, "I restored Haydee's sultanate to her and freed her from my bondage. Though I intended to wish her good luck and many blessings, and then take my leave, she bade me to marry her. I was dumbfounded and realized she loved me more than a brother or mere protector or former master. In a state of shock, I obeyed this unexpected and strange edict. She reminded me of you, when we were young lovers; and I thought that God was giving me a second Mercedes to reward me."

"So, are you in love with her then?" Mercedes says, her heart falling.

"Yes, I am. Yet she is a very traditional creature; and she told me before I journeyed to Paris that, as the new Sultan of Albania, I must also have a harem, as her father had; and since she intuited that I have always loved you somewhere in my heart, Haydee wants you to be my second wife, on the condition that, you and your children born of me will only inherit my former wealth; but the wealth and power of Albania will belong to Haydee's children alone. Another prerequisite is that you love and treat her like a younger sister or daughter, and that you do not attempt to dominate all of my attention or affection. She, as my first bride, will hold the position of first wife."

Mercedes replies, "I am in a state of shock, so let me ponder your words. Please, Edmond, let us return to the ballroom – I wish to be among others."

Mercedes and Dantes return to the ballroom, Ali trailing them loyally. Mercedes secures her veil over her face once more, and Dantes takes her arm to steady her steps. Their entrance holds the attention of the room for only a few moments, before all eyes move from the veiled woman and the Count of Monte Cristo, to Countess G descending the magnificent staircase. The Countess G looks disheveled, and as she approaches Dantes, he gestures for her to halt and joins her on the ballroom floor. He notices the deep red mark on her neck and asks, "Have you looked in the mirror?"

"No," she answers. "Am I not myself? Have I changed in any way since our – encounter?"

"Yes," Dantes answers; his voice is serious but his eyes are dancing with amusement. "Your eyes are glazed, and you have a noticeable bite on your neck. I would hide this mark until it heals – perhaps with a scarf, or a necklace."

Countess G dashes to the mirror and, realizing she hadn't merely dreamed of the exciting bite, slowly returns to ask the Count of Monte Cristo, "Does this mean I have turned?"

"No," says Dantes, "but if you visit me in my palace in Albania in a fortnight, I will teach you what you will need, should you have undergone any metamorphosis by that time."

Before Countess G can reply, Dantes bows politely and returns to Mercedes, and the pair enjoy several hours of dancing. Though their words are lost in the murmur of the crowd and the swish of ball gowns, it appears they are rekindling something that has long lain dormant within both of their hearts.

After midnight, Dantes approaches Countess G, thanking her for her hospitality and complimenting her on her grand new abode. "Stay out of the direct sunlight. Au Revoir, dear Countess," he says in closing. He presses his lips to her hand, as he bows and makes his exit. Though he is disappointed to have not met Alexandre Dumas, as he had been promised by the Countess, he still counts the night a success.

To Mercedes' surprise, Dantes drops her off not at her own doorstep, but at the posh Paris Princess, telling her that the royal suite of rooms is hers for the night. He assigns five servants to wait on her hand and foot, and tells her that Paris' premier milliner and dressmaker will arrive tomorrow to indulge her every sartorial whim. As Dantes is taking his leave, Mercedes says, "This cold spring night has chilled me to my bones. Even the dancing has not warmed me."

Dantes tells Ali to fetch the concierge, who appears in a moment. Dantes says, "Monsieur, please give the following order to the maitre d' to brew a night-cap, using these ingredients: 1 cup apple cider, 1 cup red wine, 1-1/2 cups pomegranate juice, 2 sticks of cinnamon, 1 whole orange peel, a dozen whole cloves pierced into the orange peel, and 6 ounces of Cointreau. Using these ingredients, combine the cider, wine, juice, cinnamon, and clove-pierced orange-peel in a sauce pan. Warm at low heat to about 180 degrees. Strain into 6 mugs rimmed with cinnamon and sugar, then add an ounce of Cointreau to each of the six mugs. Garnish with pomegranate seeds.

"Let the chef keep one cup and bring the other five cups up while they are still steaming."

"Yes, Majesty," replies the concierge.

"Will you stay then, oh majestic Edmond, to be warmed by the delightful brew?" asks Mercedes.

"You said earlier you need time to sort out the strange thoughts dancing in your head," Dantes says, "and I have work that I must complete tonight."

"Oh my dear Edmond, are you rushing back to unfinished business with your captivated Countess G?"

"No," says Edmond, "the unfinished work involves the girl I left waiting near the altar two decades ago."

"You will work for me, in the middle of the night?" questions Mercedes. "If you are willing to do that, please, share the decadent hot toddies with me. Then leave me to finish your work, so I can fully appreciate how you have made me feel like a queen tonight, as I float into the dreamiest state of mind, free of any fear or regrets."

BOOK II COUNT VII

DANTES WAXES ELOQUENT

THE MORNING AFTER, MERCEDES AWAKES feeling youthful and invigorated. The flavor of the delightful nightcap she shared with Dantes is still dancing on her taste buds.

After her appointment with the finest dressmaker in Paris, Mercedes dresses for horseback riding, as Dantes has requested, and finds him with two black Arabian beauties in the courtyard of the Paris Princess Hotel.

While Dantes helps Mercedes mount her stallion, she asks, "Can we ride on horseback as far as Marseilles?"

"Our servants will follow with whatever we need, and you can ride in the coach, if you tire; or, we can race home alone."

They enjoy the balmy spring atmosphere, as they take in the scenic surroundings throughout the greening countryside.

"Have you kept your promise to watch over my son, Albert?" Mercedes asks.

"He has already received two promotions into the elite Zouaves."

"The Zouaves?" asks Mercedes. "Perhaps that is why he stopped writing to me. He must have little free time, if he is training with that regiment."

"Yes, the Zouaves are a tribal confederation of Kabylia members of a French infantry unit. It is composed of Algerians wearing brilliant uniforms and conducting quick spirited drills."

Excited to learn this, Mercedes blurts out, "He must look handsome, dressed so brilliantly."

"You mean like his father, Fernand, the Count de Morcerf?"

"No! Albert is nothing like his father. Not in mind, soul, countenance, or deeds. Fernand's first consummation of our marriage was his last – after that I barred him from my room, and he was too prideful to force himself upon me again. He took advantage of me at my weakest point, after your father told me to give up waiting for your return. When Albert was forming in my womb, I thought only of you. In that sense, he is your child!"

Tears begin to roll down her face, as they had two decades earlier on her wedding day, and in a choked-up voice she says, "I never was in love with Fernand, and I only married him for the sake of my unborn son, so he would not be a bastard."

Mercedes continues by asking, "Can we erase the name of Fernand from our minds? If I accept to be a wife in your harem, will you accept Albert as your son and treat him like one?"

"I have already begun to do that. Here, read this letter I brought from Albert. I read it with his permission. He wrote to you that quote, 'The Sultan of Monte Cristo treats me like I am his own son, and he makes me feel like he is my real father. I believe Heaven has preserved him to bless our lives and for us to bless his.' So you see, Mercedes, you are in good hands."

After Mercedes' tears of grief turn into tears of joy, the reunited couple arrives at a lush meadow, where Ali has ridden ahead and laid out a delicious picnic. The pair feast on roasted pheasant and dried fruits mixed with wild Spanish chestnuts, enjoying the peaceful countryside and lush vegetation. The meadow is beautified with cuckoopints of yellow-green spathe covered by arrow-shaped leaves, punctuated by tiny purple flowers. Napping on a Persian rug, they become lost in the moment. They resume travelling and for days do not say a word, till they arrive at La Reserve to enjoy Turkish coffee and coconut macaroons at the Cercles des Phoceens, where they read Le Semaphore newspaper.

Mercedes says, "I can't find a newspaper these days that does not reveal some new rumor or revelation about the exploits of the Count of Monte Cristo. I'm seriously considering your strange marriage proposal. I'm not saying 'yes,' but if I do agree, it will have to be on the condition that Albania grants me a monopoly on growing hemp. I've started a business inventing and creating hemp products, and I wish to retain a modicum of independence. I've found that I have grown to like some small power over my own being, after a period of solitude. Can you agree to these conditions?"

"Yes," says Dantes, without hesitation. "But you can't let anyone know you are not subservient to the Sultan of Albania, for political and religious reasons. I cannot have my friends or my enemies thinking I am weak, for the former would lose respect for me and the latter would attempt to take advantage of me."

"Oh, you! The Sultan of my heart! I – not be subservient? That isn't the right word. I will sin by worshipping you, instead of God. You, like God, destroy only as a god could; and then, in a way only God could, save my life! You are my savior!"

"So," Dantes says, "we will marry then?"

"I will give you my answer tonight," promises Mercedes, "but why are you not anxious to read your father's letter?"

"Fourteen years in prison taught me patience. Did the coconut macaroon satisfy you? Are you ready to take me home?" asks Dantes.

As they approach Dantes' old home, Mercedes says, "Edmond, I'm beginning to feel butterflies in my stomach. I thought that only happened to young lovers, but it is not an unpleasant surprise to find that those entering a more golden stage of life may feel it as well."

Dantes' smile answers her statement, and she realizes aloud, "Youth is eternal for those in love, and neither time nor space can extinguish the magic of that original spark."

Dantes is impressed with the charming style in which Mercedes has redecorated his apartment, and he is glad that it partially bars his childhood memories from flooding his emotions. She lights the fireplace, adding warmth to her cozy bedroom. The herbal odor of hemp incense rises to delight the senses. Mercedes opens the secret hiding place and brings out the letter, then retrieves two bottles of wine. "Your father saved these wines for our honeymoon. One made the year you were born, 1796, and one from my birth year, 1800. We can enjoy these after you read his letter."

Dantes' eyes well up with tears, as he reads the missive with astonishment, and then regret. He wishes he could ask his parents a thousand questions, and that his father had not been deprived of personally conveying his blessings. Dantes' anger toward those who falsely imprisoned him resurfaces, as he realizes how his father must have suffered in those last days alone.

He is deep in thought after re-reading his father's letter, when Mercedes returns dressed in exotic silk. She takes the letter from Dantes and returns it to its hiding place, redirecting his attention to the wine. She reads the label on the 1796 bottle. "Principle Corsini from the Corti Estate, founded 1427–Cabernet Sauvignon, Merlot and Petit Verdot, aged in French oak. Let's open this one first."

Mercedes gently pours a taste of the wine into Dantes' glass. He inhales its rich aroma before drinking, then states, "A mouth-watering medley of plum, mocha, and smoke flavors. What a rare treat my father left for us; a future the Greek gods could not imagine to plan. Let's toast to Louis Dantes."

"To Louis Dantes," salutes Mercedes, "who gave me the best wedding gift a woman could dream of. To this best day of my life!"

Passionate feelings begin to flame in their hearts as the wine dulls their senses.

The poet in Dantes begins to emerge, and he recites:

> "Mademoiselle has the velvet eyes of a gazelle
> She is as sleek as the finest vessel on the sea
> Mercedes ages better than this cabernet
> The finest wine
> Her radiance is only matched
> By Haydee."

"Let's open my birth year's wine," says Mercedes, trying to distract Dantes from his thoughts of Haydee.

Dantes reads the 1800 label, "Chateau Margaux–Founded 1784," and again inhales deeply before taking a sip. "This wine has a soft, floral character on the nose, and its palate is loaded with cassis, pure dark chocolate, licorice and black raspberry on the finish," he notes.

Mercedes encourages, "Please wax eloquent with another of your poems."

Dantes, his creativity unloosed by the wine, obliges her request:
"Love the younger wine
With its playful zest and zeal
Will the mature shine
To show me the best
Tonight opens to the mystery within
The delights my soul longs for."

Mercedes places her finger on Dantes' lips, whispering, "Yes, let me give you that delight."

"Shouldn't we marry first?" Dantes asks. "You have your reputation to consider – and France is full of gossips, as we both well know."

"Why? Certainly, as Sultan, you can make it so with one word. Yet I'm afraid by chance, fate will stop us again!" declares Mercedes.

Dantes opens an envelope on the table and hands Mercedes their marriage certificate, signed and sealed by his in-house Imam, saying, "This is the work I did for us last night. We've been on our honeymoon all day, but I couldn't tell you until you said 'yes!'"

Mercedes whispers, "You may now kiss the bride."

Dantes pulls her into his lap and Mercedes gently presses her lips to his, feeling they have finally fulfilled their destiny.

BOOK II COUNT VIII

THE INIMITABLE RAYMEE

LOOKING OUT FROM A LUSH OASIS, RAYMEE SEES A SHIMMERING MIRAGE. From a palatial tent, Arabian musical tones float up the scale: e f g# a b c d# e and back down, caressing her ears.

She has seen mirages before, but this one captures her imagination.

Raymee swings between two gnarled trees, and she plucks a plump, sugary date from one of them, popping it into her mouth. A rare cloud begins to gather over the mirage, which slowly takes the shape of a man riding on a camel and steadily grows to the size of a mountain.

"Now what are you dreaming about, Raymee?" asks her cousin, Mumad.

Surprised, Raymee says, "My rescuer," pointing to the mirage. "I see him riding across the dunes to take me away from this place, and make me his queen."

"That is no savior, Raymee, you foolish girl; that is a treacherous sandstorm!" Mumad shouts.

Grabbing her hand, he quickly drags her to her father Abram's tent. She pulls away, smacking at his hand, and instead runs toward the makeshift pen, where her horse whinnies in fear.

"No time to lose!" shouts Mumad. "A monstrous fury is fast upon us." Mumad whirls around and chases the swift Raymee.

Abram shuffles to his ram's horn and blows the warning as loud as he can. He wastes no time; he knows the dangers of a sandstorm, and that the fiercest winds can flay the skin from a man. His seven wives, forty-three children, nephew, and servants all head for the underground shelter. "Where's Raymee?" shouts Abram. His gravelly voice is strained with panic – she is not only his loveliest daughter, but also his favorite.

"She is with Mumad, saving the animals," replies Rayada, Raymee's mother.

"Foolish child!" Abram swears. "You there," he points at a servant, "bring her here. Your life is worthless – her life is precious as gold. Save her, or it's your head on the morrow." The servant he had commanded glares and takes off after Raymee, though his steps are not filled with urgency.

"My servants disappoint me," Abram mutters, as he stands at the edge of their shelter and uneasily watches the sandstorm draw closer. His heart is pounding wildly by the time the servant finally drags Raymee to him; the first grains of sand are stinging Abram's face as he pulls her below ground, Mumad at their heels.

"My child," he lectures, "do not risk your life like that again. If the goats and ponies perish in the storm, I will buy you two more for every one that falls. You are far more precious than a bag of bones!"

As he lights a torch to illuminate the shadowy chamber, he sees scores of scorpions scurry into the four corners. He gestures again at the servant who had brought Raymee from the stables. "Spear those and roast them," he says. "These storms sometimes last for days – I won't have us using our stores before it's necessary." Once the scorpions are roasted, and crunching fills the chamber, Abram picks up where he had left off during the last storm, reading the famous tale of *One Thousand and One Arabian Nights*. Abram breaks off from the text about the genie and says, "We have our own Genie! Does anyone know who?"

"Raymee is the only girl with eyes like dewy violet flowers," Mumad speculates.

"Yes, she is our Genie, because the Caliph of Mecca will grant us three wishes of our hearts' desire, for her hand in marriage."

"Hooey! How can that be," asks Raymee, "since he has not seen me, and I do not wish to marry him? Does he know that I eat scorpions?"

Mumad, ignoring Raymee's sarcasm, says, "I overheard that merchant, Danglars, tell Uncle that he has travelled the world over, and has never seen eyes the color of violets – like wet flowers. The ugly merchant said that the Caliph of Mecca would probably give half his kingdom, once he laid his own eyes on such a rare beauty. If you have to marry him, make your three wishes thus: 'Grant me unlimited wishes; free me to choose my own husband (yours truly); and recognize the Bedouin as tax free and sovereign.'"

"Those are noble wishes, Mumad, but I will marry neither that Caliph nor you," says Raymee. "I will marry only for love."

"Danglars will be back here with the Caliph's advisor tonight, to give his opinion," says Abram. "If the sandstorm has blown its course and they do arrive, we must give our answer. They will come bearing gifts and supplies, and they will not want to be kept waiting."

"Father, will you allow me to become his prisoner? A Caliph's harem is a prison. I love this nomadic life, and I want to find my own husband, or perhaps never marry. Will Caliph Saad allow me to hunt rabbit and quail with my falcon? No! But this is what I love to do. I refuse to be trapped, to be nothing more than an ornament!"

"Daughter, will you marry the Caliph for the welfare of your family?"

"Yes, Father, I will – I will take his hands and say the vow that binds us for eternity. Just know that before he can force himself on me, I will escape the nuptial bed and travel to a land where women are free."

"That is not the way of our people, and you will dishonor us," says Abram. It pains him to think of his daughter being unhappy, but there is the good of the family to think of.

"Father, you dishonor me by selling me for supplies and presents. Do gold and silk so harden your heart against me? Are material possessions more important than my happiness?"

"Sell you! God forbid"

"Call it what you like, but to me the marriage contract will be a sales contract and me, your property, being sold."

"Daughter, you are very young, so you do not yet understand. After you are married with children of your own, you will realize that I have done this to bless you, and you will be a joyous queen."

"No, Father! An imprisoned queen is neither full of joy, nor sovereign. She is little better than an animal, for she has no more rights than one."

"Where do you get these strange ideas?" asks Abram.

"From the books you have read to us, Father. And from being an intelligent woman. As Hamlet says, 'I could be bounded in a nutshell and count myself a king of infinite space, were it not that I have bad dreams.' My nightmare is being a queen, Father! A trapped, powerless woman."

"O daughter, your rare eyes are surpassed only by the rareness of your intellect. Nevertheless, you overreact. Your sisters would love to trade places with you and become the wives of sovereigns."

"Then tell the Caliph he may have my twenty-one sisters," says Raymee. "And let me be."

Abram responds, "They will all dance for his advisor tonight, as will you; and then he will pick the one who most pleases him. If it is you, then you must marry him."

"I will not dance for just anyone," retorts Raymee.

The sounds of the wailing winds slowly die down over the next few hours, and finally Abram, his family, and his servants emerge from their shelter. The sandstorm has inflicted only minor damage, and the livestock is unharmed. Joyous at having escaped the devilish storm largely unscathed, all begin preparations for the evening entertainment.

At dusk, the Caliph's advisor arrives with Danglars. After exchanging Salem-a-lakems, Abram introduces the travelers to his favorite daughter. Holding his hand open toward the gentlemen, he says, "This is the Caliph's advisor, Dr. Omar, and the merchant, Mr. Danglars."

Abram motions to Raymee to remove her veil, and she reluctantly does so, revealing glowing golden skin, a cupid's pout, and astoundingly violet eyes. "Excellencies, I'm proud to introduce to you my beautiful daughter, Raymee. Are her eyes not as dazzling as you could have imagined?"

Omar says, "Seeing is believing; Danglars impressed upon us the otherworldliness of her beauty; but never having seen a violet flower, it was hard to visualize the color he described. Danglars, I must say, you did not exaggerate her beauty, and you will be rewarded generously."

"As I predicted," says Danglars, thanking Omar for his appreciation.

Abram smiles, pleased with how the conversation is proceeding, but his smile fades as Raymee speaks out of turn. "Can you place a value on me now? How much am I worth?" she demands.

The three men look at each other, dumbfounded. None can look Raymee in the eye.

"The Caliph could have my twenty-one sisters for the same price you set on me. Am I truly worth so much? And Mr. Danglars, what is your commission for finding me?"

Abram, embarrassed, responds, "You may judge the talents of my other daughters, who are ready to dance for you after the feast. One of them may please the Caliph as well."

"Are you sure this girl is a virgin?" Dr. Omar whispers to Danglars, his voice filled with embarrassment at broaching such a delicate subject. "I've never heard any girl so outspoken."

"If the Caliph wants to unravel the mystery of my virginity, he will have to first win my heart; but he shall have my love only after I turn his heart into my slave," proclaims Raymee.

Abram's face turns bright red as he says, "Noble gentlemen, please don't be dismayed at my daughter. I have indulged her mind far too much, and filled her brain with fairy tales. Let's now enjoy the entertainment and refreshments, and we will discuss our true business at a later hour."

After the dancing begins, Raymee crawls into her hiding place behind the tent, a habit she began twelve years earlier at the age of five, and one that allows her to hear all of her father's conversations.

Raymee almost breaks out laughing when she hears the men discussing how shocked they are at her feisty words, and she giggles at their attempts to repeat them verbatim.

Her attention is caught by Danglars' stories about the Count of Monte Cristo; she has heard of the book and been eager to read it. She hears him say, "And I know 'tis true, because I was a part of it. It happened just as Dumas says. Since the book was written, this Monte Cristo has emerged as the Sultan of Albania; but he isn't any ordinary sultan, as he lets Haydee, his sultana, run the country while he travels the world, up and down the silk routes, from there to China, where he feasts upon exotic delicacies, such as bird nests. I've heard he is currently staying at a caravanserais in Turkey, headed in this direction to meet his Majesty, King Saad. His second wife, Mercedes, who I met when they were children, demanded and was granted a monopoly on growing and producing hemp, which I have samples of here." Then Danglars hands the samples and a copy of that famous book to Abram and says, "Please accept these gifts, although I wonder if you should read that book to your daughter, Raymee. It seems she has enough ideas for a woman; don't fill her head with any more."

"Thank you," says Abram, "I will read it with great interest, knowing that you are a part of the story. And I will be sure to keep it from Raymee. You are right, she knows too much for a young woman."

"What is this delicious, fatty meat?" asks Danglars, who has by now dug into his plate with enthusiasm.

"I am pleased you like it," says Abram. "It is a specialty of ours – the hump of the camel."

Danglars chokes, as if he is trying to keep his food down.

"Would you like to try our roasted scorpions?" Abram asks. "They are quite tasty, as well."

"No, thank you," says Danglars firmly, "I'm quite full now. Let's discuss Raymee's bridal price. We want to be fair."

"Gentlemen, there appears to be a complication," says Abram. "My daughter has solemnly requested that she be given a year to decide; and she would like the Caliph to visit her here before that year is up."

Raymee gasps, and then covers her mouth with her hand, hoping they have not heard her. She has requested no such thing – her heart warms, as she realizes her father is trying to delay her marriage day to preserve her happiness, even if for only a short time.

"This is unheard of," says Dr. Omar, "and a great insult. The Caliph will not be treated like this."

"Please do not make any decision in haste," Danglars says. "We can do this the way it is done in France, with Abram signing a contract betrothing Raymee to the Caliph, with the terms of the contract and the date of the wedding set for one year. What are your demands for the dowry?"

"I'm thinking fifty of each of the following: camels, bags of salt, and bushels of dried fruits, grain, spices, and coffee."

"Is that all?" asks Danglars.

"Not in one day, but spread out over ten years," answers Abram. "To provide prosperity for my family, should something happen to me."

Omar says to Danglars, "Draft the agreement," and adds, "I believe his Majesty will sign that contract."

As he is preparing to leave the next morning, Dr. Omar is approached by Raymee, who requests that her private letter be delivered to Caliph Saad. Inside, it reads: "If you really want to take my hand in marriage, and for me to become a willing bride, you must write to me a letter, stating why you would be a good husband, and how you can make me happy. I understand the advantages of being a queen, but for me, that is not enough – you must persuade me in a different manner."

"O clever daughter, what did you write?" asks Abram.

Answering his question with her own, Raymee says, "Do you think that charlatan will open my letter?"

"Why would he invade your privacy? He seems an honorable man."

"He is a poor man pretending to be rich. Can't you see how desperate he is to sell me, to earn his finder's fee? You have to admit, though, that he has shown himself to be a shrewd man by creating imaginary value out of the color of my eyes," replies Raymee.

"I have a surprise that I know you will love, Raymee."

Pretending not to know, Raymee shows great excitement when Abram presents a book larger than the Koran.

"Will you start reading this book to us tonight, Abba? We don't need to finish *Arabian Nights* for the umpteenth time, do we?" Raymee asks.

"Yes, tonight, my bold and fearless daughter, we will begin."

"Are you sure it is good for a girl like me?" Raymee asks slyly. "It may give me ideas."

Abram smiles and winks at her, acknowledging that the two of them now share a secret.

Night by night they work their way through the new book, until finally a messenger arrives with a letter from Caliph Saad.

Raymee grabs the letter and runs to read it in private. It starts: "Greetings of Peace and Joy, dear Raymee. Like you, I love stories, and those stories have enabled me to travel the world without leaving my palace here in Mecca. I wrote a poem for you about how melancholy this autumn is, as I wait to meet you; and although you have never experienced it, I trust you have heard stories of how leaves turn from green to hues of gold, brown, tan, yellow, and red, as the year draws to a close. Have you imagined how strange and beautiful that metamorphosis must be to behold? The poem I wrote for you is entitled 'Melancholic Autumn,' and is dedicated to my love for you.

> 'Good morning sadness
> Sadness is a friend of melancholy
> You know the road that will take you to happiness
> So that you will not be sad or melancholic anymore
> November – the month colorful autumn leaves are all around
> The first snow falls fresh and light
> Like your soft face
> Your cheeks on the first cold morning
> Red like the roses in May
> The description of your visage is always near my heart
> You are still a young suave girl
> With eyes like wet violets
> Your hair is autumn red
> But your visage is not melancholic like autumn
> Yet like the smile of paradise
> Sweet and suave like Venus of the ocean
> A sweet divine creature
> Made of strawberry milk and petals of rose flowers
> Perfumed with spring air
> As autumn returns every year

It seems less melancholic with you on my horizon
Yet calmer and happier
The winter, spring time and summer are good friends
of autumn
The other seasons will be happy to welcome autumn's
smile again
No more melancholic autumns for me.'"

Raymee looks up from her letter, exuberant, as she hears a messenger telling of the Albanian Sultan's famous caravan heading for Mecca, expected to pass by Abram's oasis.

"Have you met this Sultan of Albania?" asks Raymee, tossing her letter aside.

"Yes!" exclaims the messenger. "You can't believe his inventions, or the dramatic performances his entourage puts on nightly. It is the very height of entertainment."

An idea takes root in her mind, and taking her father aside, Raymee says, "Father, I have already begun to make the Caliph's heart my slave." She retrieves her letter and hands it to her father.

Abram reads the letter and is astonished at how Raymee has been able to bend the powerful Caliph to her will; and he is further astonished when Raymee drops her next great idea.

"I think I'd rather marry the Sultan of Albania. If he comes here, can you make that proposal?"

"How can I?" Abram asks. "I already signed the contract for your betrothal."

"But Father, can't you find an excuse? Maybe the Sultan will give a better dowry, and make a better husband. With this Sultan of Albania, Sinbad the Sailor, I will not be a prisoner. I have heard how he treats his women, and they have their own sovereignty."

Abram replies, "You may not like him; and I may never see you again, if you go all the way off into that foreign land. Besides, he might not be greedy like the Caliph, and may be quite happy enough with his current wives. We have no Danglars to sell him on the rareness of your beauty."

"Leave it to me, Father, my intuition will know the way to his heart."

"Daughter, the book might not be true, or the man may have changed."

Raymee ignores his warning, as is her headstrong way. "Father, please send out scouts to make sure he doesn't avoid us on his way to Mecca. Did you hear that Sultan Sinbad has a floating city waiting for him at Jappa? That is the Iblis ship he is said to have commandeered from the famous pirate, Medusalocks; and he has turned it into a luxurious yacht so big that it is like a small city. I'm dying to see it."

BOOK II COUNT IX

DESERT OASIS HOT SPRINGS

NOW, AS DANTES APPROACHES A FORK IN THE ROAD**, he hears an inner voice say, "Our destiny is to the left, turn left."

Startled, he concentrates and hears more thoughts in his inner ear, surreal feminine whispers. He mentally questions, "What destiny? Who are you?"

The answer comes in that other-worldly, inner voice, "In the direct line of the progeny from Abraham through Ishmael is a man named Abram, who will accompany us to Shechem, where I will further reveal myself to you, and we will find oneness. He and one of his daughters are a part of our plan."

"What plan?" asks Dantes under his breath.

"Wait and hope for the plan to unfold, naturally, in due course."

"Who are you?" he asks again.

"My name is 'Wisdom.' I am your true mother, your parental principle. Only I reveal noumenon and phenomenon, cause and effect. Phenomenon is without form and void, yet our thoughts move upon my visage of all elements, declaring, 'let there be enlightenment and there is enlightenment.' We see that the enlightenment is good, so we call it the first dawning stage of stable consciousness, which brings about peace and progress."

"How can I hear you, yet not see you?" asks Dantes.

No answer comes, so he thinks he might be hallucinating. In this deepest part of the desert, the stars shine more brightly than Dantes has ever before observed, and the austere beauty of starlight on sand touches his imagination.

The full moon appears on the horizon, and shines upon an approaching camel.

The man riding thereupon shouts, "Ho! Good tidings of peace. I come in the name of my master, Abram, ruler of the nearby oasis. He invites you to rest and refresh under his hospitality, if you are the Sultan of Albania."

"I am he," says Dantes, "and glad to accept the kind hospitality of your master, Abram. Please lead the way."

While they travel, two burning questions occupy Dantes' thoughts. How did Abram know that he was traveling nearby, and how had that strange inner voice known of Abram? Dantes decides to act like this coincidence is of no consequence, choosing to leave the mystery alone for the time being.

When he reaches the oasis, the sight astounds him – luxurious silk tents, topped with waving flags, stand alone in the desert. Between the tents, white-robed servants bustle, and the rich smell of roasting lamb fills the air.

The man who approaches him from the largest tent is tall and gaunt, with a shock of white hair, but he moves with a slow authority that marks him as the master of the oasis.

"Sultan Sinbad," he exclaims heartily, "welcome to my home! Come, come, dismount; I will introduce you to my wives and daughters later, but for now you must relax in our healing waters."

"Water flows in the middle of the desert?" Dantes asks in disbelief. "This I must see."

Abram leads him to a natural hot spring that bubbles up from a small grotto sprouting from the sand, and Dantes sits in the bubbling water as he enjoys the cool evening air.

A young lady, veiled, places her feet in the water next to him, whispering, "Enjoy this delicious date, my Lord," and gently presses the fruit to his lips. "Your beard has grown very long since you became Sultan of Albania."

Dantes inquires, "How can you know that?" The woman's voice is warm like honey and smooth as silk; he hopes her face is as beautiful.

"My father read us the big book, *The Count of Monte Cristo*, and nowhere did it say you had a long beard, except when you escaped from D'If prison on that fateful night, and then you cut it the next day."

"You are the daughter of Abram?" inquires Dantes.

"One of twenty-two; my name is Raymee, ending with a double 'e' like that of your favorite wife, Haydee. I don't think this is an ordinary coincidence, and I am sure you being here is but a step along the path of our mutual destiny."

"That book doesn't say Haydee and I are married, so who was it that told you this and gave you the book?" Dantes questions. "How is it you know so much about me, and I know so little about you?"

"It was one of the characters in the book – he was recently here, and he was an excellent source of information about you. Can you guess which one?"

"Ah-ha! Danglars!" declares Dantes. "The other candidates from my tale are either dead or in an asylum; there is no one else it could be."

"Yes! And that same Danglars is trying to earn a finder's fee for helping my father sell me in marriage to the Caliph of Mecca. I am a damsel in distress needing a clever prince, or comrade of your caliber, to rescue me. If you can save me, my prayers will be answered and I will be forever in debt to you. Can you deliver me from the fate of the harem prison awaiting me?" asks Raymee.

"You won't be the first girl I have delivered from an unwanted betrothal. And as charming as you are, how can I say No?' Is there another man you are already in love with?"

"Perhaps, but I can't say yet what his name is, so please don't press me further. A lady should never reveal her true love, if she's not sure he returns her sentiment. Do you promise?"

"Very well, enough said. Trust me to keep your secrets."

After a few minutes of silence, Dantes notices a hawk perched near the hot springs and comments, "I have just such a hawk. Does your father hunt with it?"

"No," replies Raymee. "That is my hunting partner, Zingi. Do you bring your hawk on your journey?"

"Yes, I always do," Dantes says. "My servants were several miles behind me, and should have already arrived – one of them has the raptor in his keeping. Would you like to pair our birds of prey for a hunt in the morning?"

"Would I? I would love to," Raymee says with excitement. "In fact, that is one of the reasons I don't want to be locked up in a harem, because I would miss this life of hunting and freedom."

"Perhaps I can persuade Caliph Saad to give you more freedom, by explaining to him how my wives run their own affairs and businesses, with total freedom," replies Dantes.

"That might help, if I decide to marry him; but for now, I have no plans to do so. I do not love him – how can I, a man I have never met?"

Just then a shooting star streaked across the sky, so bright it seemed as if they could reach up and catch it in their outstretched palms. Their jaws dropped, as they looked at each other in awe, each taking a deep breath.

"What a wondrous sight," whispers Raymee. "Do you think this sign is a symbol of our new friendship, marking the importance of our meeting?"

Dantes, his mind still wrapped up in the glory of the firmament, agrees. "We must indeed take this omen seriously. In the future, it may guide some significant decision we make together."

At that moment, as their eyes meet through her veil and a warm feeling flutters between them, Mumad approaches with an angry expression and says, "Raymee, your father is looking for you. What are you doing here?"

"Cousin, I am checking on our guest, the Sultan of Monte Cristo, the same one we have heard so much about. Please see to his needs, while I say goodnight to Father. Goodnight, cousin. Goodnight, Sultan. Mumad, will you go hunting with us in the morning? His Majesty has his own hawk."

Sounding less agitated, Mumad says, "Oh, is that what you were discussing? Certainly, include me. I will be ready at dawn."

Sinbad wonders if this Mumad might be Raymee's true love, but he doesn't sense that type of chemistry; yet it is clear that Mumad is in love with Raymee. He can see it in the looks Mumad gives Raymee when she is not looking – half full of longing, half angry that she does not notice him in that way.

Raymee sashays off, well aware of the picture her slim figure makes in the moonlight. After she goes, Dantes rises from the hot spring and begins to dry himself. When he is fully clothed once more, he reaches into his pack and pulls out a brass object, topped with a glass globe. He fiddles with a knob on its side, and the object soon produces a bright light. Mumad, captivated by what he thinks may be magic, asks, "How do you make that lamp burn so brightly?"

Dantes responds, "I created in this lamp a small upper chamber full of water and a smaller lower chamber, filling it with rocklike calcium carbide. This valve lets the water drip into the calcium carbide at a steady rate. When the water makes contact with the carbide, it develops acetylene gas, which I set to be directed to a nozzle in a parabolic reflector, which you noticed I lit manually. I can keep this lit continuously for days. See if you can blow it out."

Mumad blows as hard as he can, but he cannot extinguish the flame.

"Allah Akbar!" cries Mumad. "Your invention is magnificent." He is impressed with this interloper despite himself, and feels a secret worry inside – with such a man around, how could Raymee ever care for her cousin, instead?

*   *   *

Later that night, Dantes sets up his telescope. Exploring the infinite night sky, he feels a tap on his shoulder and hears a silken voice ask, "May I look at Venus, please?"

"Oh! Hello again, Raymee. Let me find Venus for you. Though it is bright enough to be seen with your eyes alone, it is truly a different experience when viewed through the telescope."

Pulling open just enough of her veil to look through the telescope at Venus, Raymee says, "I don't see any ocean up there. The Caliph of Mecca wrote in his poem about the Ocean of Venus, so why can't I see it?"

"Perhaps the Meccan Caliph was referring to a goddess, the Venus of Greek lore playing in earth's ocean," observes Dantes.

"Oh; that must be the meaning," Raymee declares. "I'll have to read it again, with that in mind."

Dantes looks at her curiously. "So, the Caliph writes you poetry? I have heard from your father that you are to wed him within a year – he must be a romantic man."

"I have never met him," answers Raymee. "I wish he had never been born. I do not want to join his harem, and give up my freedom." Her violet eyes blaze through her veil. "It would be worse to me than death. Yet I struggle – I must fulfill my father's wishes and do my duty as his daughter. If I disobey his wishes and do not marry the Caliph, I will have shamed my family. If I honor his desire and wed the Caliph, I will have shamed myself."

Dantes looks at her in sympathy. "I, too, know what it is to struggle with one's desire versus one's duty," he says. "Perhaps it will all work out for you yet. Do not lose hope, my lady."

The next morning, as they travel out to hunt with Mumad, Dantes continues to watch Raymee, and feels sympathy for her in his heart. She is beautiful, and seems as virtuous as she is lovely. And so educated – her intellect could rival that of any well-to-do young lady in Paris.

The afternoon's entertainment is a makeshift production of Hamlet, performed by Dantes' crew of servants, who have an astounding knack for acting.

After watching the dramatic play, Raymee says to Dantes, "If I did not know better, I would think all of your servants high-born gentlemen and naturals of the stage. I admire their talent greatly. May I act as Ophelia in the next performance, and test my own?"

An idea sparks in Dantes' mind, and he speaks. "We will perform for Caliph Saad, if your father will let you travel with us; and we can invite your father, as well, since you will of course need a chaperone."

"Will you leave regardless?" asks Raymee. "Are you determined to travel to his lands?"

"Yes," says Dantes. "We leave tomorrow morning. Are you not eager to meet your future bridegroom?"

"I will go with you," says Raymee, not answering his question. "I will convince my father – he rarely refuses my requests."

That night, Abram puts on an elaborate feast for Dantes, and each of his daughters dances before him – each lovelier than the last.

Raymee sends Mumad on an errand, just before she changes into one of her sister's belly-dancing garments. She admires her flat stomach and lush curves in the mirror, before she returns to the feast.

Abram is surprised, when he realizes that it is Raymee behind the veil, dancing around Dantes in a most seductive manner. He has never seen her dance for anyone before – she has always refused. Her moves are so provocative and sensual that Abram blushes, and Dantes feels his heart start to pound, as the luscious woman before him whispers, "It's me, Raymee," and then smacks his ear with a kiss before dancing away once more.

Dantes looks around to see if Mumad has witnessed Raymee's shameless display, and he is relieved when he sees Mumad is not present.

Trying to distract himself from the heat he feels radiating throughout his body, Dantes turns to Abram. "I have enjoyed your company, sir, very much. I hate for our time together to end so soon. Will you accompany me to visit the Caliph of Mecca?"

"Yes," answers Abram, without hesitation. "Raymee has already asked that she might go, and I cannot let her go unchaperoned. I also cannot bear for her to be disappointed, when I know she is already distraught over her nuptials."

"Could you also guide me to Shechem?" asks Dantes. "I need a reliable source to take me through these vast deserts."

"Certainly," replies Abram, "that is where my forefather Abraham, the father of my ancestor Ishmael, communed with God. Muhammad appropriated unto himself, for the Arabs, my ancestors as their own, and ran Ishmael's true offspring out of Mecca. We practice the original religion and way of life of Ishmael, as taught by Melchizedek, who blessed and taught Abraham. Raymee marrying Caliph Saad could bring my offspring back into power in Mecca, which is why I am so adamant she obey me in my choice of a husband; but even the Caliph is ignorant of the fact that the true heirs of Ishmael were run out of Mecca hundreds of years ago. What do you seek in Shechem?"

Dantes answers, "This may be hard for you to believe, and indeed it will make me sound mad. But I have heard a strange voice in my mind, and it directed me to you and then to Shechem."

"Ah," says Abram. "The still, small voice of mystery, heard by Abraham, Moses, and even myself. That same voice told me that through one of my daughters, the twelve princes of Ishmael will arise. In a night vision, I witnessed the rise of the great princes throughout Arabia. What else did that voice reveal to you?"

"The inner voice told me that she, for the voice I heard is feminine, is my true mother, and that only through her wisdom comes enlightenment; and that she reveals both cause and effect," replies Dantes. "She has said that she will reveal more in Shechem. Why Shechem?"

"Shechem is an important place for divine revelation," explains Abram. "Recall that Jacob wrestled with that same inner voice over there. Now that I know you also hear the voice of wisdom, I am even more convinced I must guide you to the Caliph, and then beyond his lands, to Shechem."

In the morning, Dantes, Abram, Mumad, and Raymee, together with their caravans, set out for the long journey to Mecca.

Though Dantes has known Raymee for only a few days, he begins to feel strangely taken with her. He reasons that his long and lonely absence from Haydee and Mercedes has made him vulnerable to Raymee's flirtatious charm, and cautions himself against falling in love with her. She is already betrothed to the Meccan Caliph, a powerful man whom he should not like to have as an enemy; and furthermore, his new friend Mumad is also under her spell, and Dantes would not be a honorable man were he to step in and try to take Raymee's heart for his own. These thoughts trouble Dantes at each encounter with Raymee, as the journey proceeds.

BOOK II COUNT X

RAYMEE'S REVENGE

AT THE HALFWAY POINT OF THE JOURNEY, THE CARAVANS come to a halt. As Abram and Dantes' servants set up camp, Dantes spots an approaching tribe of bandits. Though they appear far away, it is only a trick of the desert light, and the bandits are quickly upon them.

"I will handle them," says Abram. He takes a horse and rides to them, stopping their determined march. When he reaches the group of motley-looking men, who he notices are armed to the teeth and have a desperate, hungry look in their eyes, he asks, "What are your demands?"

The ruler of the riffraff rudely says, "Willingly give us your possessions, including your women, and we will spare your lives, granting your men one camel to return home. We will also leave you your canteens. You do not want to anger me – the wrath of Shayton is as fearful as that of Allah."

Abram says, "Give me a moment to convince my people. I will return in a few moment's time." When he reaches the encampment once more, he stiffly swings down from his horse and motions Dantes into the large tent they've set up.

Abram consults with Dantes, asking, "Do you have weapons? Are your men trained to fight? That will be the only way to deal with those ruffians – they are savages, and will not negotiate or listen to reason."

"Yes to both," says Dantes. He turns to Ali, who is always at his side, and says, "Sneak out behind this tent and stealthily prepare the paralyzing blow-darts. On my signal, which will be a curse on each bandit, starting from the chief, shoot one of the men. Don't let them see you, so they will think I have supernatural powers. Abram, go back out and tell them that your Imam wishes to have a word with them; this will gain us a little time."

Dantes slips into a set of Abrams robes before he exits the tent, then greets the bandits. "Gentle ruffians, I beseech you in the name of your master, Shayton, to reconsider the dire consequences of your demands. As you know, Shayton will not forgive your failure."

The bandits break out laughing, as their chief, a monster of a man, says, "I am that master, Shayton; and you will find us to be murderers, rather than mere ruffians, if you test my patience longer."

"I warn you, Shayton," threatens Dantes, "I possess the power to strike you down just by pointing my finger and saying a simple curse. I warn you not to test *my* patience!"

Again the bandits break out laughing. They do not notice Abram toss a scorpion onto Shayton's saddlebag.

The horses begin to grow restless. Feeling the tension in the air and thinking that Ali should now be in place, Dantes issues his first curse, pointing his finger. "You, Shayton, will be hexed forever, if you do not now repent!"

Just then, Shayton feels a scorpion bite his leg; he lets out a grunt and then grabs the scorpion, smashing it on the handle of his saddle. As he eats it raw, spitting out the barbed tail, he scoffs, "Is that your best curse?"

The bandits resume laughing. When they have calmed, Dantes points to Shayton and says, "You are condemned to die now, fall off your horse dead."

Shayton's eyes grow wide with shock as he reaches for his neck, and falling to the ground while his horse darts away. At first, the bandits think their master is joking, but when he fails to rise, Dantes says, "Which one of you is brave enough to challenge me now?"

The bandits look at each other in fear, and quickly ride off after their master's horse. They leave their slain leader in the dust.

Abram claps Dantes on the shoulder. "You are a wise and brave man," he says. "Would that I had you for a son-in-law!"

Raymee overhears her father's praise, and smiles to herself. "Perhaps you shall, Father," she says quietly.

That night, Abram throws a big feast in celebration of Dantes' heroism in saving their lives, and Dantes dedicates his bravery to Raymee. "When there is such a beautiful woman to protect," he toasts her, "it is easy to act without fear." He sees how his chivalry pleases her, and again tells himself that she can never be his.

As Dantes begins to doze off to sleep that night, he hears a whisper in his ear. "It's me again – Raymee. Are you awake, Sultan?"

She lays herself on top of Dantes, face to face. She then sits up, wrapping his long beard around her fingers, pulling his chin toward hers. Bending forward, she presses her lips to his – it is her first kiss, and it sends a thrill to her toes. She is sure the Caliph could never light such a fire inside of her.

Dantes whispers, "But you are betrothed to someone else, and my friend Mumad is in love with you. What are you doing?"

"Shhushh," whispers Raymee. "Close your eyes. You are not responsible for what happens here tonight. I am a very head-strong woman."

Dantes whispers, "I'm crazy about you, yet I've never clearly seen your face. It is always covered with a veil – how I wish that I could look upon you."

"You can see my face with your hands." Raymee takes Dantes' hands and puts them under her veil. "Are these features not beautiful to you?" Then, moving his hands under her shirt, she presses them to her naked breasts. "Are these not succulent enough for your lips?" she asks, pulling his head against her. "I am yours."

Dantes is unable to withstand her advances, and he is surprised the camp manages to sleep through their passion. As she rises to go, she says, "The Caliph has only daughters now, as none of his wives can produce sons for him. With your help, which you have just so generously given me, I will produce a prince to be ruler of Arabia."

Dantes is amazed and a bit bewildered, but he falls back to sleep easily, spent from the intensity of their lovemaking.

Finding her way back to her own bed, Raymee discovers Mumad, his face pale with shock. She sees in an instant that he knows she has been with Dantes, and she is furious.

"Why have you destroyed me?" Mumad demands. "You know I have loved you forever. I would die for you and sacrifice everything for you. You only think you love him because he is famous, and you love the stories of him, not the real man. I have been beside you your entire life, watching over you, and yet you waste your virtue on a stranger!"

"I love him for the reasons you have stated, and for reasons of my own," says Raymee. "I cannot control my desire for him."

"Then I can no longer control mine," declares Mumad, grabbing her arms in his strong hands. "I will take you by force! I have waited long enough for the moment you so freely gave to the Sultan tonight."

Freeing her right arm, Raymee slaps Mumad across his face as hard as she can, hissing, "Very well then, you said you will make any sacrifice for me. When we arrive in Mecca, I will call on you to make that sacrifice, and you will become closer to me than a husband. Tell me now, yes or no, because I will give you no other option for this opportunity again."

"Yes," agrees Mumad, hurt in his voice. "I agree to any sacrifice as my solemn oath, though you are no longer my childhood friend and love, but some new creature I barely recognize."

"Because you have taken the solemn vow from which I will never release you, you will get to know this new creature better than anyone, just as you knew my childhood self better than anyone. Just be patient, Mumad. I am a woman of my word."

They both go to bed with anger in their hearts, but Raymee has a plan, as well. In the morning, she waits for Dantes to awaken and leave his tent, then hurries to his side. In the distance, they both notice the vultures beginning to feast on Shayton's corpse.

Dantes rubs his hand over his eyes. "Was I dreaming last night, Raymee?"

"It had no more importance than a dream," Raymee says, coyly. "I could never compete with Haydee for your heart, and I will not steal another woman's husband. I will never settle for being second in a man's heart. Yet, can I escape my fate? Will I betray my destiny?"

"What is your fate?" asks Dantes.

"Did you already forget the dream? I am to give birth to the Prince of Arabia and a whole line of great princes. Was the dream so bad that you should want to wake up from it and forget it happened?"

"I must confess, my dear Raymee, that I have only had a few experiences in my life so exciting, and none that were such an unexpected pleasure. I've felt your face and beautiful body with my hands, and experienced the greatest joy a man and a woman can share, and now I long only to behold your face with my own eyes."

"The time will come, my dear Sultan, but it is best for you to seem genuinely surprised when that moment arrives, and only then you will appreciate how cunning I truly am. Can you teach Mumad to play the part of Ophelia's brother before we arrive in Mecca?"

"That depends on his willingness," says Dantes.

"You certainly can count on that, dear Sultan."

Raymee is right, and Mumad is an eager student, learning his part well and quickly, as the day approaches when they are to perform for the Caliph.

As the caravan arrives in Mecca, the stage is set literally and symbolically for the play and events to unfold.

All are in awe as they enter the Caliph's realm – he lives not in a silken tent, but in a large stone building, impressive in both height and design. He greets them warmly, having heard of their approach from his own watchmen, and he grants them the nicest rooms in his palace.

"But you will not rest from your journey until you have performed!" he declares, not a man who is used to waiting for his pleasures. "I have heard from afar that your productions are not to be missed, and I will have you perform several times before you continue your journey."

Abram and Dantes sit next to the Caliph of Mecca, as the play begins. The voice of the actress playing Ophelia catches the Caliph's attention, and begins to closely watch her, noticing that she gazes at him throughout all of her parts. He is so captivated that as soon as the show ends, he demands to have the young lady brought before him and asks her, "May I see your face? Please remove your veil."

"No, Your Majesty, I can only show my face to my betrothed, and I have not yet decided if he is worthy of my love. He has passed two tests so far; first he wrote me a beautiful poem, and second he found my voice attractive; less important, though still a requirement to win my heart, is that he is handsome."

"What a strange coincidence, as I have recently written a poem to my betrothed to prove myself worthy," says the Caliph. "Can you quote for me a line from the poem you were sent, or tell me what it is about? Perhaps I can model my next verses upon it."

"First, let me ask you a question," says Raymee. "If that girl for whom you wrote the poem made it a condition of marriage that she have the freedom to choose her own eunuch, and own her own private residence, and take her hawk hunting when she likes, would you grant her those three wishes?"

"If her eyes are really as irresistibly beautiful as I've been told, yes!" says the Caliph. "I would not hesitate to give her everything she desires."

"And would you marry her tomorrow, if you beheld her violet eyes tonight, and would you grant her supremacy over all of your wives, if she bears for you a son?"

"Yes! Yes! Yes!" exclaims the Caliph. "Are you Raymee, with the violet eyes? Please do not keep me in suspense any longer. Abram, is this your daughter Raymee? I would not have expected you to bring such a precious jewel across the desert. Sultan Sinbad, does this actress have violet eyes?"

"I can't say," says Dantes, "as I have never seen her eyes."

"Young lady, may I know your name?" asks the Caliph.

"Before I remove my veil," says Raymee, "I respectfully request that His Majesty, my future husband, make a vow to me, that he shall always honor, cherish, love, and respect me, and carry out my will as if his own for all of his life. Are you willing to make this vow?"

"Yes, anything to see your violet eyes! Please, I beg of you. Kindly remove the veil." The Caliph is overwhelmed with desire, for he is a great collector of rare jewels and objects, and a girl with violet eyes would be the crown jewel in his collection.

The suspense is palpable, and all attention is focused on Raymee, as she slowly begins to remove her veil. Then she stops, saying, "I need a token of your love. What can you give me as a show of your sincerity?"

"I have these three brilliant diamonds; please accept these as a token of my sincerity to love, honor, respect, and adore you, and to serve your will as if it were my own, forever. Will you accept this token and my pledge?"

"Yes," says Raymee, "and I will choose my eunuch now. Bring my cousin Mumad here."

"But Raymee," exclaims the Caliph, "you promised to remove your veil!"

"I will in a moment," she says impatiently. "I will need clear vision to see my first act as queen in my new country."

"What act is that?" asks the Caliph.

"Have your guard strip my cousin Mumad on the stage, and have your physician remove his testicles while your guards pin him down."

Mumad cries out, as the veins in his forehead swell. "Please – don't!"

An evil grin spreads across the face of the Caliph, who says, "So ordered!" as Abram and Dantes watch in horror.

The Caliph looks at Raymee and says, "Wait, Dr. Omar, don't cut yet – Raymee must remove her veil."

Mumad begins sobbing, begging Raymee to forgive him and spare him this indignity. The spectators are torn between catching a glimpse of Raymee's eyes and the gruesome operation about to occur on the stage.

Dantes says, "Wait! Raymee, how can you justify such cruelty? Mumad is your childhood companion, and he loves you with his whole heart."

"I was too ashamed to tell anyone," Raymee says, hanging her head, "but Mumad tried to force himself upon me one night on our journey. I freed myself only because my panic gave me strength, and every night since then, I have been unable to sleep, fearful he would return in the night."

Dantes' eyes go hard and his face becomes a mask. "I have no further objection. Proceed."

Raymee removes her veil, and all eyes are trained upon her. The Caliph drops to his knees and kisses Raymee's hand, saying, "Mine eyes have come to see the meaning of paradise. This must be the same feeling Adam felt when first seeing Eve in the Garden of Eden. Allah Akbar."

Although not quite so enraptured, Dantes catches his breath, when Raymee's eyes meet his for the first time. Then Raymee says, "Proceed with the castration."

Mumad's squirming and crying make the horrifying events even more terrifying, as Dr. Omar finishes the job and turns, bloodied and holding the symbols of Mumad's manhood. He says, "Should we preserve these in formaldehyde?"

"Yes," Raymee answers, as everyone else remains stunned by her coldness and cruelty.

Dr. Omar whispers something in the Caliph's ear. Raymee, overhearing Dr. Omar once again questioning her virginity, holds up her hand to quiet the crowd before her. "Dr. Omar, I see you still doubt my purity. For this insult, I demand that you be my second eunuch. So that there is no question, let me ask Mumad, do you hate me for depriving you of your manhood?"

"Yes," cries Mumad.

"So, if I ask you a question, you will answer it honestly, in spite of this hatred? Keep in mind that if you lie, I will next have your tongue removed!"

"Yes!" cries Mumad.

"Have you seen me every day since we were babies?"

"Yes!"

"And did you fall in love with me?"

"Yes!"

"Did I ever give myself unto you, or did you ever succeed in forcing yourself upon me?"

"No!"

"Was I a virgin when Dr. Omar came to visit and insulted my father by questioning my purity in front of me?"

"Yes, but I didn't hear him question your chastity," says Mumad.

Dr. Omar says, "See, this witness clears my good name. I have not questioned Raymee's maidenhead."

"Accept your fate, Doctor. You cannot escape it, and if you lie again, I will have your tongue, too, and I will keep it as a trophy to look upon every day to remind me of my power. I will produce two witnesses against you. Father, did not this doctor question the sanctity of my fidelity to my betrothed?"

"Yes," Abram says, horrified at the thought of what that confirmation spelled for Dr. Omar.

"Now, my husband, you are the other witness. Will you tell the truth, and thereby condemn your friend to being my second eunuch?"

"But your Majesty," says Dr. Omar, "she is not yet your wife and she is already calling you her husband. Please let me check her privately, as a doctor."

"There!" Raymee exclaims, "He has witnessed against himself in front of everyone. The only one who will see me privately is my husband, and if he confirms the doctor's fears, he can have my head. Guards, secure this man here on this stage, so that he is naked, with nothing in reach but his scalpel and blades.

"Once he castrates himself, the marriage will be consummated. He is to be given no food or water until he has done as I command. If his Majesty becomes impatient to take me in my bed, then he may personally conduct the surgery, but no one else may touch this man."

Everyone in the room looks at each other in shock, except the Caliph, and as an evil grin overtakes his face again, he says, "Now-now, good doctor, be a good sport, and don't force me to be the one to take away your manhood, as I am not a skilled physician."

"I beg forgiveness for my indiscretion," cries Dr. Omar, realizing that he is trapped.

"I cannot," says Raymee. "Your opportunity disappeared when you said, 'See, this witness vindicates me,' which made you more than indiscreet; it made you a false witness, guilty of perjury."

"How do you know such erudite legal terms?" asks Dr. Omar, "and why not take my tongue, instead of my testicles?"

"To answer your first question, my mother Wisdom taught me what I know; and to answer your second, because I demand your humiliation for the humiliation of my father's honor. And even if he will forgive you, I will not," says Raymee.

Dr. Omar looks at his bloody hands, his tools, and his naked private parts. He cannot fathom the horror of what he knows he must do.

* * *

During the sumptuous wedding feast later that evening, a whole goat is roasted over an open fire of wood imported from Persia, and servants bring out platters of dried fruit cuscus, lemon-zested tobuli-salad, and eggplant baba-ghanoush. Dantes asks Raymee why she acted so vindictively toward Mumad.

She says, "Let's enjoy this pistachio-stuffed date pie first." Sipping on mint tea, she finally begins to explain herself. "I learned from your life story that I had a 'Fernand' on my hands, and my measures were not vindictive but rather protective; first, to kill his insistence on becoming my husband; and secondly, to keep him from harming you or me."

"But, poor Dr. Omar – that is certainly revenge," replies Dantes. "I cannot reconcile the sweet girl I thought you were to this cold woman you have become."

"There are good reasons for my actions," says Raymee, "but I will reveal only one now, and that is that these people only respect raw power. My performance tonight will put enough fear in them to enable me to control them."

"I see the logic in that, and I also know how sweet revenge first tastes," Dantes concedes. "Yet, I must warn you that revenge always recoils on its victor; and this, you know, I learned first-hand. Be careful, Raymee. The fruits of revenge are not always as pleasing as they look hanging upon the branch."

The End

If you enjoyed Book II, please "hope and wait" for Book III to be made available soon.

Enjoy the opening verses to Book III Count I, as a sample of what is to come.

ENTERS SHERLOCK HOLMES

THINKING I HAD written the last account of the adventures of Sherlock Holmes, it comes as quite a delightful surprise when London's most celebrated detective calls on me one beautiful spring Sunday morning, in the twilight of my retirement.

"My dear Doctor Watson," declares he, in a voice charged with a newfound gusto and electrical energy, "There is one last adventure from my youth that must be recorded for posterity."

"What posterity?" says I, "Neither of us have children."

"That is a different story. But we may circumnavigate the world to get back to that adventure of mine, too. However, the posterity that I reference is that of the Count of Monte Cristo, his heirs, and all of those that his life has touched. More precisely, I am referring to our literary posterity."

"I read the book with great interest, and the subsequent news reports of how he rose to become the magnificent Sultan of Albania. But how can an adventure from your youth reach to so famous a persona without my knowledge? How can you keep such a singular secret from me all of these years?"

"'Singular,' most definitely. We can even call this case, 'singularity itself,' as this is the case whereupon I cut my teeth discovering my investigative powers, which shone more brilliantly than you yourself were privileged to witness through our countless adventures. What I never told you is that Conan Doyle was my best childhood friend, and his family invited me to join them on their vacation in Paris."

"You mean to say that Sir Arthur Ignatius Conan Doyle was your childhood friend, the very one that the Queen knighted recently?" Dr Watson asks.

"Yes, the very one. And he and his father play an integral role in this greatest of all adventures. What I am about to relay to you will change your perception of history and blaze a path to understanding the future."

Dr. Watson opens a box carved of mahogany wood, intricately inlaid with pearls, and offers a Cuban cigar to his best friend, saying, "Tell me if these are not the finest smokes yet."

While waiting for an answer, Dr. Watson asks, "Have you increased your dosage of cocaine? Because never have you been so electrified with energy!"

"Indeed, I am more electrified than ever, yet not from cocaine, which I now eschew. Rather, it is due to your good recommendation, and my excitement in knowing how you will respond to learning about this greatest of all adventures."

Holmes, puffing as Dr. Watson lights his cigar, adds, "This is indeed the finest Cuban to date; however, it does not compare to the smoke you recommended."

"Ahh-hah! Let me guess!" shouts out Watson. "You now stuff your pipe with Cannabis Sativa?"

"You hit the bull's-eye, my dear Watson! Just wait until you see my lab, overgrown with various strains, together with my other amazing experiments!"

"I can't wait to write down every detail. Let the story telling begin!"

ABOUT THE AUTHOR

Who is The Holy Ghost Writer?

T HE MYSTERY OF the identity of the author is part of an international contest. The first person to discover the identity of the HG Writer, from the clues found in the several Count of Monte Cristo sequels, will receive a reward of $2500.

Submit what you believe to be the correct answer to *prize@ sultanofmontecristo.com*, in order to win this reward, along with letting us know the clues that led you to discovering the identity of the author. Should the winner wish his/her identity to be known in the press, he/she may request same. Those that already know the author or have worked with him/her will not qualify. Good luck.

Lightning Source UK Ltd.
Milton Keynes UK
UKHW010628041219
354721UK00002B/30/P